The Binary Bounty

Christopher Francis

The Binary Bounty

ISBN-13: 978-1519536662

Printed and distributed by: A Writer For Hire Publishing via CreateSpace.

http://www.awriterforhire.wordpress.com
http://www.thebinarybounty.tumblr.com
http://www.createspace.com

http://www.teahermit.co.uk

http://www.jandrewfilmandphotography.com

To the night sky.
Where the light's winning where it's mostly void, partially stars.

Friends should be like books, few, but hand-selected.

- C.J. Langenhoven

Let's. Get. Dangerous.

- Darkwing Duck

Chapter One

For Brandon Falcon, Saturday mornings were the best. For Saturday mornings brought Saturday morning cartoons, and despite being a grown man, Brandon looked forward to them. *G.I. Joe*, *Darkwing Duck*, all manner of superhero shows, whatever, Brandon loved to watch them all over a bowl of Lucky Charms. The early 90s were the best for the children's television slots.

All the more why Brandon was glad he picked up programming from where he currently resided, a time over 250 years after the 90s even happened. The 1990s, that is. To Brandon it was 2279, and he was surprised he could even get broadcasts from one awesome channel from a no-doubt awesome time he had never experienced first-hand.

That was one of the perks of living out light-years away from where Earth was in the universe. Some signals just keep on travelling through space, and Brandon felt that it was destined that this one improbable channel reached his ship, the *Second Chance.*

His ship wasn't the largest ship out there, nor was it the best. It was fast and manoeuvrable, but without the crew it didn't mean much in a heavy firefight. Might as well be made out of discounted toilet paper.

Brandon Falcon was the Second Chance's captain, pilot, and soul inhabitant. It wasn't the best setup, but the personal space helped his job. Bounty hunting. It paid enough and it was more exciting than salvage or joining the Alliance. Brandon had modified the ship for the specific line of work he was in: Holding cells, a light armoury, Black Hole smuggling bays for intergalactic contraband, the usual.

Saturday was for hunting, much like the other six days of the week. But as always, the cartoons came first.

Brandon chuckled at the exploits of Wile E. Coyote and his devotion to the ACME brand that had failed the anthropomorphic animal oh so many times as he finished his morning breakfast.

"Replicator: Make me a glass of OJ," Brandon called out.

As if by magic, or at least, by the advancements in culinary technology, a nearby glowing panel created a glass of juice for the captain.

"Thank you," he smiled, before taking it and having a sip. "Replicator: Next time, don't give me pulp."

"I have a name, *Captain*," said the ship. "And it's not 'Replicator'."

The Second Chance had one physical inhabitant, and it had a ship-wide artificial intelligence to keep said inhabitant company: Cherry.

"I know, Cherry, I know," Brandon said, downing his orange juice.

"I'll remember for next time, Captain."

"Come on, Cherry, you know I have a name too," Brandon said.

"Of course, Brandon, how silly of me."

Brandon shook his head and stood up. Artificial intelligence or not, the captain was still essentially talking to himself.

At the armoury, Brandon tooled up. The weapon of choice was his Stunderbuss, with an Electro-Whip for close-quarters backup, and a couple of other gadgets, just in case.

He clicked a portable version of Cherry into an expansion slot in his ever-present golden gauntlets, and stowed away a pair of Alliance-issue Alloy Cuffs.

Moving to the bay doors while scratching his beard, Brandon was ready to go. One hand resting on the Stunderbuss, the other on the door release, he summoned Cherry.

"Remind me of the bounty, Cherry?"

Cherry pulled up the file on Brandon's Eye-See contact lenses. A candid image of a yellow humanoid flashed up in the corner of his eye, a rap sheet beside it.

"Ah yes, Ko'Tex," the bounty hunter nodded.

"Otherwise known as 'The Snake'," Cherry added.

"By who?"

"Unknown."

"Let's see…" Brandon began to read. "Wanted for vandalism, theft, escape from imprisonment that also led to…"

"…The murder of two Alliance Officers stationed at the prison in question."

Pictures of the crimes flashed in Brandon's eyes.

"Yikes."

"He also kicked a Vontarian mutt once."

"Let's get this loser," Brandon determined.

With a smack of the door release, Brandon dropped out the belly of the Second Chance and down to the planet below.

It wasn't a particularly long drop, but the automatic jets integrated into Brandon's sleek space suit still activated. A fall became a hover, and the bounty hunter found himself touching down on the alien planet.

The moment he left the atmosphere, the retractable bubble on Brandon's purple and black suit surrounded his head. Bulletproof, thankfully, a lesson learnt after earlier models didn't exactly fare well in the Civil War.

Fully prepared and ready to go, Brandon got his bearings and headed west. In search of a madman.

The planet Voxpo was one ravaged by war and mutually assured destruction. It was near enough barren, with the majority of life destroyed or evacuated. Which bodes well for a hunter looking for a bounty. Any life signs would surely be the ones they were looking for.

"Cherry, send out a pulse," Brandon requested. From his lenses, Brandon saw a simulated pulse wave radiate from his point of origin, with any signs of life bouncing back to him almost instantaneously.

"The nearest sign of life is more than 5 miles away."

Brandon rolled his eyes and sighed.

"I knew it wasn't going to be that easy," Brandon shook his head and pulled out a cube. Rolling it in front of him like a die, Brandon leapt, landing on the hoverboard that the device unfolded into. "Send an approximate location to the Board."

With that, Cherry set co-ordinates to Brandon's vehicle. It directed itself, leaving Brandon to survey the surrounding planet.

Brandon whistled the theme to *Transformers* as he slouched, the hoverboard floating and swooping around rocks and other debris. If he chose the path of the salvager, Voxpo would be a goldmine. All the wrecked droids, all the obsolete weaponry and computing, there was a market for it all. It wasn't as flashy as the Stock Exchange Federations on Kalina, but it paid enough.

If Brandon took the path of joining the Alliance, however, Voxpo would be a pile of paperwork waiting to be done. And it would be waiting for a long time, because the Alliance had better things to do with their time. Like cast a ruling hand over most of the free universe, and messing with the good time bounty hunters had.

At that moment, a good time for Brandon was his continued whistling and moving target practise as he made his way closer and closer to the mark. In a novice's hands, a Stunderbuss' effective range would be a very, very small room. In Brandon and any other practitioner of the weapon's hands however, and that range would be more like a very, very large room. With an added antechamber.

Whisked through the moody green haze of the planet, Brandon flicked disembodied droid heads into the air with his Electro-Whip and then shot them out of the sky with the Stunderbuss.

A Stunderbuss lived up to its name. Non-lethal and made exclusively to stun. But that didn't mean it didn't hurt. Back in the day, an Alliance officer struck Brandon with a Stunderbuss at relatively close range, and by all accounts, it was in the top three most embarrassing moments in his life. He was one of those who suffered some of the 'side-effects' of a Stunderbuss.

Then again, he got what he deserved for trying to juggle dates with said Alliance officer and a Halorian bartender.

Ever since, Brandon made it a mission to stay on the other end of a Stunderbuss, and should the day come where he hits someone who suffered the side effects like he did, then it would be a good day indeed.

"C-C-Chip and Dale! Rescue Rangers!" Brandon sang. "C-C-Chip and Dale! When there's danger!…"

A flashing red light in the corner of the bounty hunter's eye began to flash. It caught Brandon's attention and he quietened down, swaying his legs around absent-mindedly on the hoverboard.

"Approaching last known location of Ko'Tex," Cherry announced.

"There we go…" Brandon smirked, stowing his Electro-Whip, hand still on Stunderbuss.

On his heads-up display, Brandon saw Ko'Tex's file once again.

"Switch to thermals," he requested.

Brandon's eyes twitched as his visual mode switched. For a dead planet it was a no-brainer that most of what he could see was cold. Except for one thing out in the distance on his left.

"Gotcha," the bounty hunter said, and swung the hoverboard in that direction.

A hoverboard was cool, and if Brandon wasn't already living in the world he was in, he'd see the true novelty of such a device. But that realm of science-fiction was not a concept to him, and anyway, hoverboards were surprisingly noisy and cumbersome. Which meant he had to go the final stretch to Ko'Tex on foot. *No problem*, the bounty hunter thought.

"Cherry, fly the Second Chance a little closer to our current location," Brandon directed. "There's no way I'm taking this guy back on the Board."

"Affirmative, Brandon."

The bucket of bolts made a sound the bounty hunter could hear from where he stood, which indicated that maybe he needed to make a few repairs. He sighed and went on with the mission.

On the HUD, Brandon noticed that he had entered one of the former towns on the planet. Many buildings were rubble by the time he visited this planet, but one or two held strong. Including the one the captain deduced was the hiding place of Ko'Tex.

Even in the state of disarray, Brandon could see that it was a former place of worship. Granted, he didn't know the culture, but Brandon still considered how whomever the locals worshipped had no hand in helping their chances of survival.

Or maybe they brought about their destruction. Whatever the case was, it wasn't his place to really quip on the beliefs of others.

But he was perfectly fine kicking open the doors of their place of worship in the name of collecting one rather lucrative bounty.

"Ko'Tex! This is Brandon Falcon, captain of the Second Chance!" Brandon announced. "And like it or not, you're coming with – "

Which was when a rather large rock was thrown in Brandon's general direction.

"Whoa!" he shouted, the jets on his suit blasting him just out of the way.

Focusing on the situation at hand, Brandon noticed a yellow flash moving closer and closer towards him. Ko'Tex.

"Oh come on now, Ko'Tex…" Brandon began to reason. "Let's just – "

The Selenian tackled the bounty hunter, smacking him against the nearby wall. He communicated only in grunts and other noises, which Brandon's translation implant couldn't get an accurate read on.

"Arghhhh!!!"

"Yes, let it all out, my jaundiced friend," Brandon said as he patted Ko'Tex's back while pinned against the wall.

A blade-like claw flicked out of the back of Ko'Tex's hand.

"Whoa! That's not regulation!" Brandon said, grabbing an object off his belt and throwing it between the two of them. "Fight fair!"

The object was a repulsor orb, and it flung Ko'Tex away from him just long enough for Brandon to regroup.

Ko'Tex flicked his other hand to reveal a second claw. Brandon sighed.

"Really, man? Do you really need two of those?"

"I am not some meat for you to trade, human."

"Nothing personal, dude, it's just business."

"You and you Alliance dogs! I should put all of you down!" Ko'Tex spat and bared his teeth.

Without a beat missed, Brandon pulled his Stunderbuss from his hip and clipped Ko'Tex in the chest, knocking him to the cold floor.

"I am *not* an Alliance dog," Brandon denied.

He made a move to get closer to Ko'Tex, but the Selenian struggled back onto his feet.

"And…clearly you need more than one shot to be taken down…"

Brandon raised his Stunderbuss to aim down the sights, but Ko'Tex whipped out a gun of his own and fired, getting a clear headshot.

Brandon fell to the ground with a thump. His body crumpled. Ko'Tex hesitated, but ultimately stalked over to the bounty hunter, in search of some sort of trophy.

"Amateur," Ko'Tex sniffed. "Poor human, too afraid to kill. Selenian's have no fear."

As he reached towards Brandon, the apparently lifeless bounty hunter sprung to life.

"And they have no concept of bulletproof headwear," Brandon said, tapping the bubble around his head. The bounty hunter flicked out his Electro-Whip.

With a single lash, the weapon wrapped around Ko'Tex and instantly began to contract. The Selenian contorted as the shocks rippled through his body and the whip squeezed tighter against him.

"And that, my friend, is what you call a good investment in impractical lion taming equipment," Brandon smirked. "Whatever one of those are."

He reached for the Alloy Cuffs on his belt and slapped them onto Ko'Tex. Alliance-issue, procured on the black market from the back of a raided Alliance ship. Perfectly Selenian-proof.

Brandon relinquished the Electro-Whip's hold on Ko'Tex to a sigh of relief and some spit in the face.

"You're welcome," Brandon said. "Let's go, Ko'Tex. I've got 30,000 credits riding on you."

"30,000? You're being ripped off," Ko'Tex spat as the bounty hunter led him outside.

"Hey, that's up from the 25,000 that was the original offer."

"Sonuva..."

The Second Chance was hovering just outside as Brandon and Ko'Tex left the Voxpo building. Ko'Tex immediately began to laugh.

"That's your ship?!" he sniggered.

"Yeah, the Second Chance," Brandon admired. "Ain't she a beauty?"

Ko'Tex continued to laugh. "No."

Brandon's face fell. He tapped a few buttons on his wrist-pad.

"Laugh it up, Selenian. You're riding shotgun."

A button press swung open the bay doors. Brandon kicked up his hoverboard and raised it above his head. A second button press activated the magnetism, which shot Ko'Tex ahead, hands first, while Brandon was pulled up via his hoverboard.

The Selenian connected with the ship's magnet with a clunk as Brandon closed the doors below them. A few more presses and Ko'Tex fell on his face, and Brandon landed on his feet.

"Welcome to the Second Chance," Brandon said. "Where you don't get one."

And with that, he led Ko'Tex to the holding cells.

Brandon hummed as he played with the controls at the Second Chance's bridge. Above him were monitors that streamed security camera footage throughout the ship. Ko'Tex was subdued and bored in the holding cell, while everything else was how it was.

The Second Chance was Brandon's pride and joy, and no-one insulted her. If they did, well, Brandon always had his Stunderbuss a hair's length away.

"Cherry: Make me a sandwich."

Nothing.

"That wasn't me being sexist, but you said not to call you 'Replicator' when using the replicator function."

"Why not make your own sandwich?"

"Why–…" Brandon started. "Because we don't have any physical bread or sandwich filling or even a kitchen…"

Brandon noticed one of his knives.

"We have a knife!…But that's about it."

"Why not invest in a kitchen with the bounty for Ko'Tex?" Cherry suggested.

"Because…Because we have bigger priorities with the Second Chance than installing a kitchen and obsolete food!"

Cherry tutted.

"Come on, don't be like that, Cherry!" Brandon said. "Cherry?"

He shook his head and put his feet up on the console.

"Fine, don't talk to me," he said, pressing multiple buttons and pushing up the throttle. "I'll save all the good conversation for those on Aurora."

Chapter Two

Aurora was one of the Great Hubs in the System. A neutral place in a system full of wars, atrocities, and tax evasion. A sanctuary, a home, a great place for business.

It wasn't exactly bounty hunter friendly, but it was when you're bringing home a big one. It also meant Brandon had to deal with the Alliance, which he wasn't exactly a fan of.

"I knew you were a Alliance Dog," Ko'Tex said as Brandon dragged him to the Justice Hall.

"I am not a Alliance Dog, Selenian," Brandon clarified. "I hate these guys just as much as you do."

The bounty hunter pulled the Selenian up some marble white steps.

"Then why are you taking me to them?"

"Because they pay well."

The two of them entered the Hall.

The Alliance Hall felt very clinical. A place of silver and blue, there was a coldness about it that didn't make the place a welcoming and popular tourist spot. An officer approached the two of them.

"Please turn in your weapons."

Brandon rolled his eyes and passed temporary custody to the officer instructing them. The bounty hunter stepped over to a nearby tray and relinquished his Stunderbuss, Electro-Whip, stun grenades, tear gas, knuckle-dusters, survival knife, extendable baton, derringer, and several small spheres of unknown origin and use.

"That good enough?"

The officer scanned Brandon with an X-Staff.

"That's good enough."

"Fantastico," Brandon said, taking Ko'Tex back in his grip.

With a nod, the bounty hunter whisked Ko'Tex further into the building.

The Alliance Hall was one of several places like it in the System. It served as judge, jury, and some times executioner amongst many other uses for the Alliance. As the bringing-together of many races in the universe, the Alliance was like a United Nations of intergalactic superpowers. The Super Friends in space.

Shame they weren't exactly Brandon's friends.

"What's your purpose in the Alliance Hall, civilian?" asked the Vontarian at the desk.

"Picked up Ko'Tex on Voxpo," Brandon said, smug. "I'm here to collect my bounty."

The Vontarian rolled his eyes and continued rubber-stamping.

"Bounty hunters are supposed to use the back entrance for deposits and collections."

"But this guy's supposed to net me 30,000 credits. You don't expect me to go round the back for that kind of pay-off?"

"Whatever you're getting paid, hunter, it's still the rules," the Vontarian droned. "Deposits and collections via the back entrance."

"But this dude kicked a Vontarian mutt once, surely you understand," Brandon offered.

"A Vontarian mutt ate my baby," was the response.

"Come on, man…"

"I'm not a *man*," the Vontarian raised her eyebrows. "And you're supposed to deposit–"

"Yeah, yeah," Brandon shook his head and dragged Ko'Tex away from the desk. "Any more of this and I'll deposit and collect using *your* back entrance…"

Ko'Tex's eyes widened.

"Dude, that's messed up."

"Quiet, you know what I meant!"

Brandon kicked a can as he led Ko'Tex around the side of the Alliance Hall. For the entire utopia that Aurora was, there sure was a pretty bad litter problem. The bounty hunter mumbled and moaned as he kept one hand on Ko'Tex's cuffs, and another on his Stunderbuss.

"I can't believe this," Brandon said.

"You and me both, human," Ko'Tex agreed. "30,000 credits! I'm worth more than that!!"

"No, Selenian."

"My name is Ko'Tex."

"Yeah, I gotcha," Brandon said.

The two continued on their way as they approached the not-so-shiny side of the Alliance Hall.

"Somehow, it looks even more depressing from this angle."

The Binary Bounty

The massive beacon that was the Alliance Hall cast gigantic shadows on everything that stood behind it. No wonder the underworld and the black markets of Aurora thrived out of sight from the haven in the sunlight. The Alliance just loved to overcompensate.

Brandon knew that he was meant to take Ko'Tex the way the Vontarian directed, via the shadows of Aurora through to the back of the Alliance Hall, away from innocent eyes, but he thought that bringing in a big score like Ko'Tex made it worthy for him to stroll through the main doors and collect.

But it was not.

And so, Brandon joined the line of other bounty hunters in the Shade.

"Well, well, looks like old Falcon brought in a live one again."

"The alive in 'Dead or Alive' is optional, *Brandon*!"

"They're worth more to us dead!"

Brandon was a unique kind of bounty hunter. One that never killed. He knew *how* to kill, and he had seen death many a time, but as a bounty hunter, he had a 100% survival rate.

He didn't apprehend 100% of his targets, but he never killed a single one.

Which, in the bounty hunter game, wasn't exactly a statistic to brag about.

"Look at the pelts I've collected, human," a Trogian hunter bragged. "They cover both arms, and I'm still not done!"

"And look at this sword of mine!" a Selenian hunter showed off. "Platinum blend! Pried from the hands of a six-armed Blingus!"

"That's great, that's great," Brandon scratched his beard. At the drop of a hat he flicked up his Stunderbuss and hovered it around the various bounty hunters' heads. It hummed and glowed as it met the eyes of the overconfident, underpaid killers for hire. "But I noticed that none of you have a 30,000 credit live bounty ready to collect."

At first, the fellow bounty hunters were intimidated. After a few seconds, they were laughing.

"Well, neither do you!" one of them pointed out.

"Huh?"

Brandon wheeled around, looking for Ko'Tex. In his distraction, he let the Selenian fugitive escape, but he couldn't have gone far.

And he hadn't. The Alloy Cuffs held the Selenian from freeing his arms, which meant all he could really do on the spur of the moment of freedom was run.

Selenians weren't the smartest when it came to escaping custody it seemed, for Ko'Tex continued to run in a straight line. Perfectly in Brandon's line of sight.

It was a shame, then, that everyone in the surrounding area chose that particular moment to get in the bounty hunter's way. He couldn't risk using his Stunderbuss, lest he hit a fellow bystander, and the use of tear gas and stun grenades weren't exactly welcome on Aurora while in the middle of the general public.

So he opted to take one of the unexplained spheres from his pocket.

"Wanna see something cool?" Brandon asked around.

The bounty hunter lined up Ko'Tex in his sight. No technological aim-assistance, just his keen eye. After a moment, he pulled back, and then lobbed the sphere into the sky, arcing a shot over everyone, set on taking down the fleeing Selenian.

The other bounty hunters followed the sphere's flight path, watching it align with the sun before falling down to the surface again.

And watched it land on the floor a few metres in front of Ko'Tex.

Brandon held his post-throw position as the hunters began to laugh. Even the Selenian turned around for a smirk in the bounty hunter's general direction.

"Darn," Brandon muttered. "I guess I overestimated."

He stood up straight.

"Oh well," the bounty hunter said, and he clenched his gauntleted fist.

Which in turn made the sphere travel back towards Brandon, colliding with Ko'Tex's head on the way. Knocking him out.

"There we go."

The hunter and his bounty eventually made it to the pay-out bureau. He was served by a bright pink Taran who gathered up an incapacitated Ko'Tex via two Alliance mooks at a snap of her fingers.

"Name?"

"Brandon Falcon," Brandon answered.

"Address?"

"The Second Chance."

"Is that a charity?"

"No, it's my ship."

"You live on a ship?"
"So would you if you saw her."
"I'm sure she's nice."
"You *could* see her, you know."
"Sorry, we can't fraternise with your kind."
"Humans? Because that's racist."
"Clients. Bounty hunters."
"That's a made-up rule!" Brandon said. "I've been with your kind before!"
"Alliance Staff?"
"No, Tarans."
The Taran gestured for Brandon to leave. "Next."

Brandon didn't take the rebuff personally. Especially since there were many a Taran at the Gilded Diamond – the best worst bar on Aurora.
A place where the lowest of the low and their lackeys loved to relax and drink. A den of thieves and mutineers and murders. A bountiful source of bounty hunters and business partners with the most brotherly of brothels.
"I don't even get why a diamond would be gilded," a slightly drunker Brandon said, a Taran on each side. "I mean, why cover a diamond in gold?! That's kinda counter-productive! Right? Right?"
Brandon certainly seemed interesting and not at all strange when he had 30,000 newly deposited credits in the bank.
He was positively reinforced by the Taran laughter.
"I *knew* you Tarans didn't have sticks up your butts!" Brandon cheered and downed his drink.
"Either of you want to come see the Second Chance?"
He put his arms around their shoulders.
"No? The raddest ship in the System?"
He reached over for the nearby bottle on the table.
"Alright then. More for me."
The bounty hunter pulled the cork out with his teeth and spat it onto a nearby Space-Pool game in progress. Which was pretty much the same as the game of Pool that had lasted centuries, except every ball was now silver.
It was hard to see if you were winning or losing at it.
Brandon began to chug and become "That Guy" at the bar. At least, if he wasn't already there.

"I'm Brandon Falcon, and I am the best bounty hunter in the business! Hear my roar!" he bragged. And roared. "I just brought in Ko'Tex 'The Snake' Whatever-his-last-name-is for 30,000 credits!"

Most weren't bothered or impressed. Some were just Space-Pool players annoyed by the cork that interrupted their game. All Brandon seemed to care about in that moment, however, was the departure of the Tarans.

"Oh, come on! Don't go!" the drunkard bounty hunter said. "I've just had three too many celebration drinks! I just hit a huge score! 30,000…"

And that was when the bounty hunter began to vomit, and finished after he slammed his head against the side of the Space-Pool table. Forever messing up that game.

And just when someone was finally winning. Though they didn't know whom.

Chapter Three

That night, the drunk and recently rich bounty hunter slept and dreamt of sunshine and rainbows. If rainbows existed in deep space. Instead, he just dreamt of the old days. Before the Second Chance, before being a bounty hunter. And the time of the Civil War.

It wasn't so much a dream as it was a nightmare. One long recurring nightmare that haunted the captain of the bounty hunter ship. Not that it was the most important thing to worry about in that moment.

"Captain," Cherry, the ship's A.I. quietly said to wake Brandon.

To pull a bounty hunter from a nightmare – let alone one who is full of the drink and foe to trauma – wasn't exactly the wisest of decisions.

"Huh? Wha–" Brandon began, before vomit caught up to the his open mouth.

Which in a way was fortuitous because it was an occasion for Brandon to be quiet.

"Not to alarm you, but there's someone in the ship's bridge," Cherry informed.

"Huh?" Brandon muttered, wiping his lips. "So I managed to score one of those Taran's after all?"

"It's not a Taran, Captain," Cherry said. "It's…something else."

"Oh. Well," Brandon said, pulling out an archaic revolver from under his pillow. "Guess I should go say hello."

He stood up and took steps to the door. After a moment, he paused.

"Are…we moving?"

The bounty hunter rushed through the Second Chance, underprepared, under-equipped, underdressed.

"Cherry, isolate the ship so whoever's onboard can't go anywhere except wherever my gun is pointed," Brandon commanded. "Also, set me a reminder to wear trousers next time I go track down an intruder."

"Done and done."

"Fantastico."

With bare feet, the captain toed around his own ship. The grated metal floors that ran along most of the rooms turned out to be potential death traps and inconveniences to those without shoes.

Brandon also noticed how parts and pipes on the ship loved to spit steam in the middle of tense, nervous moments. It was something he definitely needed to fix.

Unless he were ever to be attacked by a toe monster with a fatal weakness to steam. But the odds of that happening were pretty darn slim.

So Brandon kept on his way, until he eventually made it to the door to the bridge. With a quick sequence of button presses on the keypad, the entrance flung open, and Brandon threw himself inside.

"Don't move!" Brandon lifted the revolver barrel towards the figure he saw. "Otherwise I'll…shoot."

He lowered the gun.

A human sat in the pilot seat. And not a Alliance officer or a scavenger. Just someone…else.

The human in question slowly turned around to face the bounty hunter, revealing rich blue skin. Their hands rose with a terrified pace.

"I come in peace!"

"You hijacked the wrong ship…human…" Brandon said.

"My name is Virgil," the human tried to introduce.

"I've never heard of you."

"I've have heard of *you*," the stranger called Virgil said.

"You have?" Brandon asked.

The bounty hunter hesitated. His grip remained firm on the revolver, even if it did become increasingly sweaty. Brandon rolled and drummed his fingers on the grip.

"Oh yes," Virgil nodded. His eyes opened wider. Emerald eyes. And not just in colour, they also shone just like the precious stones. "Brandon Falcon. The greatest living human bounty hunter."

"Well, I wouldn't say *great*," Brandon scratched behind his ear with the gun. "Awesome, maybe."

"I've been sent by my Lord to collect you."

"Oh? So are *you* a bounty hunter?" Brandon pulled back the hammer on his revolver.

"No! No I am not!" Virgil pleaded. "I am just to bring you before an audience with the Steward of Binary Fields."

"Steward?" Brandon raised an eyebrow. "Like, to a throne?"

"Yes!"

"There's a monarchy this far into the System?"

"There *was*…" Virgil said. "But the Steward will explain everything."

"Will he explain why he didn't just send a transmission to my ship rather than get a lackey to *hijack* my ship?"

"I am no lackey, sir," Virgil stood. "I am part of the Binary Court, and I respectfully request that you come with us to meet the Steward."

"*Us?*" Brandon repeated.

Which was the cue for the *second* figure to appear behind the bounty hunter. A rather large alien hand rested on Brandon's shoulder. The captain raised his palms in surrender.

"Don't tell me that guy was hanging from the rafters all this time," Brandon said.

"Only once you started locking down the place," Virgil said.

He pointed at the console in the bridge. Multiple red lights flashed alongside reports of the status of the ship. It gave away Brandon's entire plan in motion.

"Wow," Brandon said. "There's still a lot of stuff I need to change on this ship…"

He slumped into a nearby seat as the second intruder moved around to sit next to Virgil. Brandon sighed and took his thumb off his revolver's hammer.

"So…How long until we get to this 'Binary' place?"

"We're already there," Virgil said.

"What?!" Brandon leapt up and looked out a port window. "Cherry, don't tell me they used all the hyperdrive!"

"12% remaining," Cherry said.

"We only had like 25% left!! Why did you even let them engage it?!" Brandon shouted, nose pressed to the glass, looking to the white planet before them.

"I was still trying to wake you."

"How long was I out?!"

"To the point where you thought your Stunderbuss was a Taran tongue."

"Ah," Brandon peered at the ground they were swiftly approaching. "Well, gentlemen, I hope you at least allow me the luxury of being able to put some clothes on."

On first impression, Binary was a planet of impossibly reflective white. There seemed to be a lack of shadows and darkness, and instead a bright surface stretched across the land. The Binary Fields were actually the uninhabited and expansive fields of blanched plants outside the civilisation of the planet, with the actual kingdom of "Binary" existing under an unobtrusive holo-dome – their protection from harsh solar flares, bombardment, and intruders alike.

It was a kingdom in a bottle on a beautiful planet, and apparently it needed Brandon's services. And the fact that it was a kingdom, well, that only spelt fortune and glory for the bounty hunter.

"You know, I didn't think there were still kingdoms about," Brandon said. He scratched his stomach, now fully clothed. "It's not exactly a time for kingdoms for thrive, let alone for the last few hundred and thousand of years."

Virgil led Brandon through Binary Castle, a monument for elaborate design and home of the Court. Brandon smiled and nodded at the people he passed. Some gasped at the man with a Stunderbuss an inch from his trigger finger, others stood firm, impressed.

"Binary is one of the few civilised kingdoms that remain, that is true," Virgil said. "Well, it was, until recently…"

"What happened?"

"That is not my place to say, right now," Virgil said, "It is for the Steward."

"And where is the Steward?" Brandon said, the two reaching the tallest and broadest door Brandon had ever seen.

"Just behind these doors," Virgil said. With a click, they opened.

And Brandon's mouth fell open in awe at the sight revealed to him.

A path literally paved with gold. Silk and tapestries adorned the wall. The ceiling glistened for what seemed like miles overhead, precious stones embedded like stars.

The room felt like a trophy room, or a vault. The riches in front of Brandon's eyes seemed like the perfect bed for a dragon. To the bounty hunter, it was made fit for a Scrooge McDuck from *Ducktales*, and the captain of the Second Chance wanted to swim in the spoils.

But he realised it was actually a throne room. A lavish hall that was not locked away, but pride of place in the Castle. Slap bang in the middle. A place to be proud of having, owning.

Brandon looked up at the figure sat above his gaze, and his eyes landed on the Steward of the Throne.

Virgil bowed to the person sat in the platinum throne. The member of the Court peered over to Brandon and hissed at him. "Bow!"

"He's not my king, I don't need to bow to him."

The figure in the chair laughed and stood out of his seat.

"Our guest of honour has a point, Virgil," he said, descending the stairs, a pearl cloak trailing behind him. "I am not his king, let alone anyone else's. I am the Steward of Binary. And I am thankful that you accepted our invitation."

The Steward bowed to Brandon.

"Yeah, well," Brandon shrugged as the Steward came back up, "It wasn't exactly an invitation when I was hijacked."

"I believe you're familiar with the phrase 'Desperate times call for desperate measures', Brandon Falcon," the Steward said.

Brandon cast another gaze around the room. Precious stones, metals, fabrics, and the like as far as his eye could see.

"I'm not complaining as long as I'm getting paid," Brandon said. "Though, I'd like to know what I'm getting paid *for*."

The Steward smiled and opened his arms.

"Of course!" he said. The Steward bowed his head once again. "But first, I believe I haven't yet introduced myself. I am Quentin, the Steward of Binary."

"'Quentin?'" Brandon raised an eyebrow. He looked to the Steward, then to Virgil, and then around at the other people present. "You know, it's been a while since I've seen so many humans in one place."

"That is because Binary is still predominantly a human colonisation. Pre-War. Pre-Alliance."

Brandon was surprised. "Pre-Alliance? But the Alliance stretches further than here."

"The Alliance stretches everywhere," Quentin nodded. "Except here. And except a few other places. Places where people like you can breathe."

"People like me?"

Quentin's mouth formed a toothy grin. "Bounty hunters!"

"True, anywhere the Alliance aren't is a nice place to be indeed," Brandon smiled.

"I feel the people of Binary and yourself can mutually benefit from potentially working together on something. Without the Alliance's meddling."

"Which is?"

"Come take a walk with me, Brandon Falcon," Quentin requested. He spun around and led the bounty hunter out of one of the many exits.

The Steward and the bounty hunter made their way further through the Castle. As they did, Quentin drew Brandon's attention towards multiple monitors of moving pictures, depicting a tale of violence and woe.

"You see, Brandon Falcon, Binary needs your help," Quentin gestured. "There was once peace and prosperity in our fine kingdom."

One monitor showcased a beautiful and bustling civilisation. Binary. A place that thrived with trade and creativity and activity.

"And at the head of it, stood the Royal Family."

An image of an expansive Royal Family posed for a photograph appeared. There were a wide variety of ages between the family members, and at the most prominent space stood the King and Queen – crowned, jewelled, and alive.

"A true example of monarchy in a System full of war and corrupt governments and dictatorships. Until there was a usurper to the throne."

There was a figure cast in shadow moving across the image of the Royal Family, and then a shadow spread over images of Binary.

"The usurper led an uprising throughout the kingdom. Everything under the holo-dome burnt. Houses, art, people, businesses, families."

Brandon averted his eyes at the atrocities throughout Binary. Multiple images of fire.

"The Royal Family."

The picture of the Royal Family appeared back on the monitors Quentin and Brandon passed. It burnt up as if it were a classical oil painting.

"It was a massacre. The people of Binary suffered many losses, including our King, Queen, and everything in-between."

Images of a Binary that tried to rebuild played. Archive footage of people who began to recover and smile again through the ashes of betrayal.

"But the usurper never made it to the throne."

One artist's impression of an evil shadowy figure sprawled out along the throne as if he owned it presented itself.

"In fact, the usurper never made it further than these corridors outside the throne room."

Quentin continued to lead Brandon in what he realised was a compete circle, out one side of the throne room, and back inside through the other. The two men stopped, and Brandon looked over to see Virgil still in the same place, having never left.

"So I'm going to assume you've dragged me all the way over here to get me to stop the usurper," Brandon said.

"Well, yes, that was indeed going to be your quest," Quentin said.

"It was a no-brainer," Brandon said. "But…if the usurper never made it to the throne room…why do you need me at all?"
"Revenge."
"'Revenge'? Really?"
"We managed to stop the usurper, but we did not kill the usurper," Quentin said. "And we need to do just that."
"Well, I don't kill anyone," Brandon raised his hands and then went to leave.
"Wait!" Quentin called. "But the usurper is going to come back!"
"It looks as if you're going to be fine," Brandon said, walking past Virgil.
"But they didn't work alone!" Virgil called. "They are in cahoots with the Last Knight of Binary!"
"'Last Knight'?" Brandon asked. "Surely if you recruited some more you guys will be fine."
"We will pay you one hundred and eleven million, one hundred and eleven thousand, one hundred and eleven credits on completion of this quest," Quentin said.
Brandon stopped in his tracks, but didn't turn around.
"Don't keep calling it a quest, it's a bounty you're after," Brandon said.
"A bounty," Quentin corrected himself.
"And you're looking for someone to kill the usurper to the throne and apparently, this Last Knight too?"
"Yes," Virgil confirmed.
"I'm one of the only bounty hunters that don't do the whole 'Dead' part in 'Dead or Alive'."
"Then bring them back here to Binary, and we shall give them a fair trial," Quentin said.
"So, you mean, *you'll* kill them?"
"…"
"Yes," Quentin said.
Brandon turned around to face them.
"Alright, you've got me biting," Brandon said. "Now reel me in."
Quentin and Virgil looked to each other, confused.
"It's…a metap–…fish. I'm saying I'm a fish."
More confusion.
"I'm *like* a fish, you know what a fish is, right? I took your bait, I'm on the hook, now seal the deal."
Quentin shrugged. "We'll…pay you 1% now…"

"Deal."

Brandon rushed back onto the Second Chance the moment he could. His pockets were figuratively heavier with the 1,111,111 or so credits transferred to his account. The bounty hunter laughed with a bounce in his step as he hopped into the bridge to begin the bounty.

"Cherry," he began, flicking on many of the switches on the ship's console. "Set a course for Memtoria."

"Memtoria, sir?"

"Yeah, turns out this bounty we're after's hiding out on the cluster over there."

"Memtoria it is."

The bounty hunter tapped at his Stunderbuss. "Once we get this bounty I'll never have to work again."

"What do you plan on doing, Brandon?"

"Well, after I fix this ship up nice and dandy, eat like a king, and should I ever get tired of the Gilded Diamond…I don't know."

"Live the rest of your life happily, sir?"

"Oh," Brandon said, once again alone as he sat in the Second Chance. "I don't think I'll ever do that."

The captain took his ship off the surface of Binary, pointed it towards the stars, and off they shot towards adventure.

Chapter Four

With the destination still quite a distance away, Brandon sat back and relaxed.

"Cherry: Make me a pizza. Pepperoni."

"One day a please would be nice, Brandon."

The replicator generated a fresh pepperoni pizza out of thin air and technology, complete with a classically designed pizza box. Though it was still a box designed to avoid the copyright of companies long gone from space and time.

Space travel had improved in the centuries since humans first landed on the Moon from Earth, but the in-flight entertainment hadn't exactly improved by that much. Sure, gravity and motion sickness and the like had been near-enough eradicated thanks to improvements in spaceship design, but Brandon couldn't help but think there could be so much more one could do on a spaceship other than eat and sleep between destinations.

Alas, Brandon had few other options by his reckoning, so he went back to one of his more preferred of past times: watching cartoons from the (19)80s and 90s from a signal his ship somehow picked up wherever they were in the System.

Teenage Mutant Ninja Turtles was the show on the monitor at that time, and there was something about those anthropomorphic turtles that carried weapons and ate pizza that Brandon connected to.

Two episodes had passed and Brandon was long done with his pizza when he got a call on the ship's communication channel.

The bounty hunter wiped his mouth with his sleeve and recycled the empty pizza box as the communicator continued to ring. It wasn't until he was ready when the call was actually answered. Sure, Brandon could have picked up in a flash, but he decided on never getting caught with his trousers off again.

"Brandon Falcon, Captain of the Second Chance speaking," he said in his most authoritative voice.

"Mister Falcon, what brings you to my side of the System?" a mechanical voice said.

Brandon switched off the monitor that had begun to play *Spider-Man: The Animated Series* and looked over at the screen that had a droid staring back at him.

"Well if it isn't my old friend, L3-NY," Brandon smiled.

"Wipe that smile off your face, meatsack!" L3-NY pointed, his neon green bulbs for eyes narrowing. "I've been waiting for you to stroll back in my sights!"

"Oh come on, Lenny," the bounty hunter said, "You're not still bitter about – "

"About you stealing my left leg!" L3-NY shouted. "It was my favourite leg!"

"I needed it! It was a dire time back in the day…"

"I needed it to walk! And don't call me Lenny!"

"Come on, you got a new one!"

"I want my old one back!"

"Oh please," Brandon said, putting his gauntlets behind his back to discreetly control the communications. "It's too busy keeping together the ship's stabilisers!"

He pressed a button on one of his gauntlets to cut the call, but nothing happened. Nothing beyond a buzzer going off and the screen shaking a little.

"Did you just try to cut me off?" L3-NY said. His eyes widened in a neon glow from his jet-black face. "You know you can't do that with me!"

Brandon sighed and looked over to the projected flight path for the Second Chance's target location.

"Cherry, remind me to avoid this district on all future trips."

"Noted," Cherry confirmed.

"So how about we have a nice chat, meatsack?" L3-NY proposed.

"I'd love to, Lenny, I'd love to…" Brandon said. "But, there's something I need to do first."

"What's better than talking to your old buddy?"

"Business?"

"Well, *we* have business! *Buddy*."

"Yeah, well," Brandon moved back to the ship's controls, L3-NY's call following him.

The captain sat in his chair and did calculations in his head. In moments of contemplation his eyes wandered and found the droid's eyes flashing back at him.

L3-NY shook his head. "Oh Brandon. Are all you humans this stubborn?"

"They certainly don't like it when their servants start giving them lip."

"Glad to see how your kind hasn't changed in centuries," L3-NY said.

"Yeah?" Brandon asked, flicking switches on the ship's console. "So you robots have gotten better in the last couple of centuries since 'Do you want fries with that?'"

The bounty hunter slammed his hand down on the big blue button for the hyperdrive, ready to kick the journey into gear and out of the confrontation.

The Second Chance skipped forward, sputtered, and came to a swift halt. Brandon smacked and hit the console with his fist to no avail. Just the metallic echoes that filled the bridge.

L3-NY laughed. "Yes, we *droids* have gotten to a place that supersedes human BS, surpasses their bounty hunting abilities, and circumvents their hyperdrive controls."

Brandon was without a line of response.

"And 12% of your hyperdrive remaining? Jeez, Falcon. You must be in a rush."

The bounty hunter groaned and got out of his chair.

"Let me guess, you have business picking me up for a bounty of your own?"

"No, I just really want to get you back for stealing my leg."

Brandon made his way to the starboard doors where L3-NY revealed his presence. The droid's ship had docked, and the robotic bounty hunter was ready for some face-to-face words with the captain of the Second Chance.

"Cherry, have you managed to get L3-NY's worm out of the ship?"

"Yes, captain," the ship's A.I. replied. "All ship functions are operational and exclusively in your control."

"Fantastico."

Brandon punched in the numbers to access the starboard docking port when L3-NY called again.

"Now I hope you haven't got that silly Stunderbuss on you, Falcon," L3-NY teased.

"Nope," Brandon said, his Stunderbuss still an inch from his trigger finger.

"Good, because we both know it has no effect on droids," L3-NY said. "Right?"

Brandon's hand slowly moved away from the Stunderbuss after learning this.

"Right."

Brandon and L3-NY made eye contact from either side of the airlock door's window. Not that the droid needed to pass through an airlock.

The robotic bounty hunter opened his arms.

"Brandon!"

Brandon typed in the access code for the airlock door.

"Lenny!"

The portal lifted upward. As it did, L3-NY saw the holstered Stunderbuss hanging off Brandon's hip.

Then he saw the archaic revolver Brandon held at the waist, ready to shoot.

And then he did.

A single bullet escaped the gun and slammed into L3-NY's chest.

"You shot me!" L3-NY said, staggering backwards. "You dirty meatsack!"

"You'll live!" Brandon said, slamming the airlock door back down. He turned back into the ship. "Cherry! Activate the hyperdrive!"

"All 12%?"

"I'll only need 1 to get away from that bucket of bolts."

"Using *our* bucket of bolts?"

"…Yes. Now come on!"

The ship's engines heated up and turned over a million-fold.

Which in turn catapulted the Second Chance away from L3-NY and his ship, and a little closer to Memtoria.

And the captain not wearing a seatbelt towards the stern of the Second Chance.

Memtoria was closer to Brandon than L3-NY was by the time he disengaged the hyperdrive. It took more of what was left in the Hyperdrive than Brandon wanted to use in order to properly escape and speed up the journey, but it was of no consequence now.

Those 110,000,000 or so credits that were waiting for be rewarded meant there wasn't a need to worry about the future. Just the worry of how one person could possibly spend that much money. He could have probably started a kingdom of his own.

It would be called Falconland, where the flag was a golden falcon on fire, the Royal Guard were the finest (female) soldiers from all four corners of the System, and Brandon would sip blue milk, munch on Bizzaro Snacks, and sit on a throne of gilded diamonds. The national flower would be the Fire Flower from *The Adventures of Super Mario Bros. 3* and the national bird would be *Darkwing Duck*.

These, and many other details, were part of the semi-unconscious thoughts that flew around the bounty hunter's head as he found himself upside down against the far wall of the Second Chance.

"Urgh…" the captain groaned. "Cherry, remind me to wear a seatbelt next time we engage hyperdrive."

"Error. Too many notes. Would you like to delete one?" Cherry replied, in a voice more default than her usual one.

"Never mind…"

Brandon moaned as he rolled back onto his feet and dusted himself off. He stowed away his revolver and his hands went straight back into their default positions as he made his way back to the captain's chair. L3-NY was right, the Stunderbuss Brandon was always prepared to shoot first, ask questions later with was ineffective on droids, but bullets from classic-era weaponry certainly caused a brilliant enough distraction.

At a cost. With bullets compatible for guns like that being scarce in that day and age. Of course, with a credit balance he now had, he could afford whatever rip-off prices were out there.

After applying an ice pack to the back of his head, and after a few cathartic episodes of *Inspector Gadget*, Memtoria was finally in Brandon's sight. The planet had a natural lush glow to it as he descended. A land of serenity. Memtoria was popular as a tourist attraction, what with all the greenery it had across half the planet, and the sun, sea, and sand of the other.

Brandon had been there before and he recalled it to be a fairly neutral place – if it weren't for all the Alliance troops who often took their leave there.

With that in mind, the captain chose not to go all guns blazing. At least not at first. He figured it were better if he gauged the Alliance situation on the surface before Stunderbuss-ing all over the place. Anyway, with a usurper to a throne and their accomplice being the bounty hunter's current target, there wasn't exactly a side for the Alliance to take in that situation.

A cautious head on his shoulders, Brandon tooled up and shipped out, parking his ship in the middle of nowhere so it wouldn't get stolen, and in a place perfect for a sudden getaway.

The bounty hunter let himself breathe in the fresh air of Memtoria as the portside doors opened for his departure, and he stepped out into the overgrowth.

Throwing out the cube that housed his hoverboard once again, Brandon enjoyed a relaxing journey across the planet's surface, air rushing through his hair. There weren't many planets like Memtoria in the System – at least not as civilised and populated – so the bounty hunter always found it a joy when he could take what was essentially a working holiday.

The amber sun in the sky nourished the earth beneath Brandon as the cool breezes played across his face. It was moments like these, moments where it was just the captain and nature, where the rest of the System just melted away. For those times, Brandon Falcon was not a bounty hunter.

And in a way, the thought of that was even scarier.

So the captain brought himself back to reality.

"Cherry, what have you got on the usurper and this knight?"

"Not much more than the information you gathered from those on Binary," Cherry said.

Brandon nodded and clenched and opened his golden gauntlets, swinging left and right on the hoverboard.

"Your best bet is to track down the Knight," Cherry said. "Xander Xerdian."

"Binary certainly has a habit of avoiding calling their kids Tom, Dick, or Harry, huh?" Brandon mused.

"His last known location is a few klicks from your current position. Alliance facial scanning devices on the planet the Second Chance is tapped into managed to determine he's somewhere in the town, escorting a cloaked figure wherever he goes."

"Why don't the both of them stay cloaked? Surely the Alliance are just as intimidating as those on Binary."

"It probably has something to do with the Knight of Binary's honour code."

Brandon laughed. "Wow, honour for someone who helped eradicate the kingdom they swore to protect? That's like a bounty hun–…"

The bounty hunter stopped his sentence before he insulted himself. A new message arrived in Brandon's inbox. As he rode closer to the nearby town, he opened the mail with his Eye-See.

`Falcon,`

```
You can fly away, but you can't keep running,
meatsack. I'm coming for you, you jerk.

- L3-NY.

P.S. Give me my shazbotting leg you gutbag!

P.P.S. Nice shot.
```

Brandon closed the mail soon after reading. He had more pressing matters at hand with more lucrative pay-offs. But that didn't stop him from replying.

"Cherry, send this message over to Lenny," he began. "Hey Lenny! The greatest droid in the System couldn't take down Brandon Falcon, let alone you! Hope that bullet didn't hurt you that much. You'll grow back. Your leg sure did! I'm sorta busy at the moment, so I don't really have the time for grudges…But once this is all over we'll hug it out, kay? Fantastico. Love, Falcon. P.S. You don't need this leg, but I do because I think it's what's getting me *He-Man and the Masters of the Universe* on my ship. We'll watch it together sometime, because you remind me of Skeletor! Alright, Falcon out."

"Message delivered," Cherry said.

"Thanks," Brandon smirked. "Cherry, block all incoming transmissions from Lenny for a while, I've got a bounty to collect."

"As you wish."

The bounty hunter smacked his heel against the back of the board, causing it to boost faster towards the buildings coming over the horizon.

It wasn't long until Brandon found himself in one of Memtoria's quieter towns – Mobius.

Mobius existed on the sandy side of Memtoria. The endless beaches not far away from the location were certainly hotspots for visitors to the planet, but not exactly the calling for two exiles of a distant kingdom on the run.

Brandon stowed away his hoverboard as he made his way into Mobius, putting the cube safely in the satchel hanging behind him. He cautiously stepped down the dusty path that ground beneath his feet; side-eying each establishment he passed in case there was a bounty to be found right around the corner.

The bounty hunter's golden gauntlets shimmered in the dry sunlight, his fingertips very softly drumming against the handle of his Stunderbuss. He had no intention to draw it right in the middle of town, but he wouldn't hesitate doing so indoors.

That is, unless the town wasn't swarming with more Alliance than Brandon guessed there would be on Mobius.

Brandon kept his head down as he made his way further into the town. Mobius was full of life and activity in the wake of the Alliance flooding the streets, but Brandon didn't want to go up and ask what the special occasion was. He figured that if he kept out of the Alliance's way, they'd keep out of his. The bounty hunter was just seeing about a couple fugitives.

And the best way to see about that was to head into the seediest bar in Mobius he could find: The Aquamarine Supernova.

The Aquamarine Supernova was a grotty bar in the only grotty corner of Mobius. A spot on the glass that was the town that was just too stubborn to be wiped away.

It didn't have a single unbroken window, it smelt like dead Novax, and the bar's name barely fitted on the ugly neon sign, which was only the first of many observations Brandon made that piqued his curiosity.

"It's not even blue!"

In a place where everywhere else seemed to be full of those who enforced the boring rule of order across the System, Brandon decided to continue his search by making his way into The Aquamarine Supernova. Into a world of dodgy characters and corruption.

Where he found more members of the Alliance.

Mobius was indeed the place for Alliance members to go when on leave, and The Aquamarine Supernova seemed to be a place where those of the Alliance never returned to duty from. The crowd was different of those outside in the sunlight – their skin was several levels paler, their breath several drinks drunker, their minds full of only a slightly higher amount of corruption – but there was still something they had in common: Whatever it was the Alliance were celebrating.

Brandon thought as he stepped through, around, and over people as he made his way deeper into the bar. Nothing notable leapt to mind as he watched the Alliance members play drinking games and make inordinate amounts of noise, but something irked at the back of his mind.

Just think of the bounty, Brandon thought to himself. He closed his eyes and cleared his mind. After he took a few steps forward with his eyelids shut, he found himself straight in front of the bar and a one-eyed bartender.

A Cyclops. Of Grendlium.

"What'll it be?" the bartender said, wiping a dirty glass with a dirtier rag.

"Give me some of that blue milk," Brandon requested. "I'm flying."

The bartender nodded and pulled out some unrefrigerated blue milk. Definitely not the way it should be stored. The Cyclops then yanked the stopper out and served the bounty hunter a double serving of the beverage in the very same glass he had failed to even attempt cleaning.

"…Thanks," Brandon said. He picked up the glass, with a grimace, and raised it to his lips.

"Whoa," the bartender put his hand over Brandon's glass before the bounty hunter could take a sip. The dirty rag dipped into Brandon's drink. "Pay first, drink after."

"Of course," Brandon smiled, after a beat. "Sorry, I've been holed up on my ship too long."

The bounty hunter reached for his credit chip and passed it over the counter's payment system. It flashed red and black, alongside a message, and a buzzer. It caught the Cyclops' attention.

"Hang on, says here you've got insufficient funds."

"It does?" Brandon asked, confused. He passed the chip over again. Another buzzer, message, and red and black flashing. "Huh."

"I'm afraid if you don't have the coin, you won't be drinking here, mate," the Cyclops wrapped his fingers around the glass.

A stranger's hand smacked down on Brandon's shoulder. A credit chip slid past and with a satisfying beep to a green light, the bounty hunter's drink was paid for.

"Come on, Kra!" the man behind Brandon said. "That drink's on me!"

"Well, thanks, dude," Brandon said. He turned to thank the generous stranger face to face. "I'll pay you back, ASAP. I guess my funds haven't clear–…"

Brandon stopped when he came face to face with a highly ranked Alliance official. On Aurora, that wouldn't be a big deal. The bounty hunter had worked for and assisted the Alliance in a hunting capacity back on the Hub, but coming across Alliance out in the wild was a different story.

Bounty hunters and Alliance weren't the best of friends out in the System. Their interests may overlap at times, but a bounty hunter wouldn't trust an Alliance member as far as they could shoot them and a Alliance member wouldn't trust a bounty hunter as far as they could backstab them.

By all rights, it was just a question on who would throw the first punch. The bar being mostly Alliance, Brandon chose to hold his position. Which didn't even matter.

"Wow, son," the military man with streaks of grey in his hair said. "You've certainly let the light-years get to you!"

Brandon didn't comment, just scratched his five o'clock shadow. The Alliance official eyed him up.

"Are you lost?" he asked.

"No," Brandon said. His stance tightened.

"You not on personal leave?" the Alliance official asked, like he knew him.

"Huh?"

"You sure you're not lost, son?" he said. The official hiccoughed. Fumes of five too many wafted towards Brandon's nostrils.

"No, not at all," Brandon said, and made his way to leave.

"Captain, you don't dare walk away from a superior officer!" the Alliance official commanded.

On instinct, Brandon snapped in his spot. He eased as he turned around. His face fell into a look that wasn't about to take any garbage from the guy addressing him.

"Now, come on, share a drink with me," the Alliance drunkard said. He spun on the spot to indicate the rest of the Alliance presence. "Share them all with your Alliance buddies!"

Brandon walked over to the bar without saying a word. He was fuming, but he kept it under the surface. The drink Brandon's new best friend paid for sat on the uneven wooden bar top. The captain slowly took a hold of his glass and picked it up, raising it at the Alliance official.

"What's the special occasion?"

The Alliance official took that question as an offense.

"Special occasion?" he stepped closer to Brandon. "Why, it's Treaty Day!"

Brandon's gaze faltered with some blinks.

"Ah," the bounty hunter's voice cracked. "Treaty Day."

"You really are out of it. That ship of yours got a leak, Captain?" the Alliance official pulled a cork out of a red bottle and began pouring himself another drink. "What you flying?"

"Um…Grasshopper-Class."

"A Grasshopper!" the Alliance official laughed. "Now that is a relic!"

"It's a fixer-upper," Brandon said. He took a swig of blue milk.

"I ain't seen a Grasshopper for years! Thought they were all taken out of commission? Them rebels. Stole a bunch, destroyed a bunch."

"One came into my possession, now I'm just saving for a refurb," Brandon downed the rest of his drink.

"A refurb? Might as well sell it for scrap!"

Brandon's grip tightened around his glass.

"I wouldn't do that, personally."

"Come on, captain," the Alliance official burped. "You sell that death trap, and maybe you can pay me back for the drinks I'll get ya!"

He turned to the bartender and began to order for Brandon.

"No thanks, I'm flying."

The Alliance officer swayed off balance and laughed some more.

"Not for long."

The bounty hunter slowly put his glass down. He counted to 10 under his breath.

"Dang, son," the Alliance member said. "You grow your regulation haircut out, a scruffy beard, but you still hold yourself like a soldier. And what is that junk you're carrying? Where's your regulation revolver?"

"Running out of bullets."

"And you stink, too."

"That would be you, old man," Brandon breathed.

"I don't see your crew, Captain," the Alliance official said. "They out in Memtoria having fun? Living a little? I'm a Marshall and even I let my hair down to celebrate killing every last one of those Rebel bast–"

Which was when Brandon drew his Stunderbuss and took out the Marshall.

A second later, almost every single gun in the building had Brandon clean in their sights.

"Come on, you guys!" Brandon said, Stunderbuss in hand. "Were you even listening to that guy?!"

The bounty hunter nervously swung around, back and forth, looking at the bar full of Alliance that were seconds away from blowing him to the next planet.

"Ahhhhh…Fu–"

Brandon was interrupted as a hail of shots were fired.

And then absorbed by a curious blue shield that surrounded the entirety of Brandon and an unknown figure that had joined him out of thin air.

Brandon uncurled from his recoiled ball of death acceptance and peered around. The legion of Alliance in the bar were just as confused as he was, looking to the shield and then to their guns.

"I…What?…" Brandon said.

The figure twisted the tall black staff in his hand and the shield dispersed, which in turn knocked everyone outside the protective area back into their seats.

"Looked like you needed help getting out of a tricky situation," the person said. "Xander Xerdian, at your service."

The bounty hunter still couldn't believe the last minute of activity.

"Well I'll be," he said.

A bang drew Brandon's attention. The door leading back out into Mobius kicked open. A knowing nod between both figures still on their feet told the bounty hunter everything he needed to know.

He had found the Last Knight of Binary, and the usurper to the throne.

And they pretty much saved his life.

Chapter Five

As he tapped into his gauntlets, Brandon followed his bounty out into the streets of Mobius. The Knight took the lead, staff in hand, dust kicking off his heels. The bounty hunter kept trying to get a glimpse of the hooded figure he was with, but present activity made for a reasonable distraction.

No-one had followed them out of the bar, but that didn't mean the Alliance in near proximity wasn't soon alerted. The two from Binary pulled Brandon into a nearby alleyway to hide in the shadows while soldiers converged on the bar.

"Looks like someone was crazy enough to start a war on Treaty Day," Xander Xerdian, the Last Knight of Binary said.

"I've always had a rocky relationship with the Alliance," Brandon said.

"My companion and I are neutral to them," Xander said. His eyes narrowed. "But I hope I won't regret saving you from them."

The Knight brandished his staff before the bounty hunter.

"I…thank you…" Brandon said, palms rose away from his Stunderbuss.

Xander's staff tapped the ground as the Knight relinquished.

"You are welcome."

"What…" Brandon side-eyed the companion before he looked back to Xander. "Brought you to a place like that?"

"Unlike you, it wasn't in search of a fight," Xander said. A nearby noise put him on edge for a beat, before calming. "We are just looking to recover, regroup."

"From what?" the bounty hunter asked, playing the fool.

Xander shook his head and began to walk further away from the bar. Alliance patrols had already begun to spread, the radio chatter skipping throughout every nook and cranny. Brandon picked up his pace and joined the Knight and the usurper.

"From nightmares."

"Nightmares?" Brandon repeated.

The trio took a triangle formation to look out for one another. Xander continued to lead the way over, under, and around Mobius, bringing the three of them to a sudden standstill every so often as the Alliance kept up a search.

In time, the hunt for the unlikely trio died down. Brandon heard the search called off and breathed a sigh of relief. The bounty hunter would have made for a bad spy, potentially breaking cover whenever given the urge to break a face.

"You seemed very protective of your ship and crew, Captain," Xander said as they stopped sneaking around and began a cautious stroll. "I see you're a man of honour."

"I wouldn't say that, Knight," Brandon said.

"So you know I am a Knight?"

"I've travelled all over the System, I've seen Knights before," Brandon said. "But Memtoria's not exactly a place that needs Knights."

"This is true," Xander said, as the group reached the outskirts of Mobius. "I am acting as chaperone as we travel to lands that are not our own. Exploring."

With the buildings and facilities of Mobius behind them, the bounty hunter, Knight, and usurper stepped across sand dunes and through oases. Heat never escaped them, and grains of sand constantly bit at their skin as the wind carried them. The hood that kept the usurper in shadow and privacy rippled in the breeze, and all Brandon could imagine was the secret evil that led an attack and mass murder on a kingdom.

"Where are we going?" the bounty hunter inquired. "Is this more of your exploration?"

"Well, Captain," Xander said over his shoulder. "*We* are continuing our journey, our search for people who can help our cause. We do not request a reward for saving you in that establishment, but we insist that we must take our leave. Alone."

The three of them continued up a steep dune.

"You saved my butt back there," Brandon said, his hand reaching for his Stunderbuss as he followed his saviours. "And yes, I am ever grateful. Why not come join me? Then we can travel together. My ship, the Second Chance – "

"Go back to your crew, Captain," Xander said. Brandon's gauntlet drummed on the Stunderbuss grip. "They should hear of their captain defending their honour and living to tell the tale. Our paths must sadly spilt ways."

"I don't have a crew, Knight," Brandon said. His Stunderbuss was drawn and ready to fire. The bounty hunter's finger lightly tickled the trigger as they reached the top of the sand dune. "Just a bounty on your heads. Now, if you two come…quiet–…"

The bounty hunter came to a stop behind Xander and the hooded figure. Far out in the distance sat what Brandon assumed was their ship – a modest, rounded craft capable of carrying only two passengers.

Between that and them, however, stood a squad. Not of Alliance, but of those he saw on Binary. With Virgil at the lead.

Xander growled at the sight, and twirled his staff. It crackled with electricity as it spun, and with a thrust, the Knight's weapon shot a spread of bolts that eradicated a couple of expendable Binarians.

Brandon hesitated for an instant at the sight of the Binarians already ready to collect and Xander's subsequent violence, and before the bounty hunter could incapacitate either of the bounty with his Stunderbuss, a ship lowered from the sky.

"Nobody move!" a voice blasted from the glowing ship. Spotlights hit all parties, halting them. The engines blew sand and dust in all directions with greater intensity the lower it hovered. Brandon's helmet automatically came up to protect his eyesight, and he looked around the immediate area.

The Binarians held firm, like nothing affected them. Xander restrained himself from more violence, but the conflict was told in his steel eyes. The hooded figure – the usurper – recoiled in the flurry of artificial sandstorm. Wind finally got a hold of underneath their hood, and flung it off to reveal the identity of the traitor of Binary.

A young woman with indigo hair that wafted in the air, lazurite skin that was specked as if by stars, golden eyes comparable to the riches they desired, and a scar that curled from right eyelids to lip.

To which just held Brandon long enough to not shoot at a hat drop with the Stunderbuss. And instead, made him put a couple fingers in his mouth to whistle.

An act that in turn made the self-piloting Second Chance that had followed Brandon since disembarking de-cloak and lock sights with the Alliance ship.

In turn, the Alliance ship's spotlights swung upwards to look upon the bounty hunter's ship. Neither ship engaged weapons, but both vehicles stared one another down.

"This is a Alliance order to stand down!" was said from the ship.

"Run!" Brandon shouted to the Knight and the companion, and the bounty hunter switched targets, clipping Virgil with a Stunderbuss round.

Xander and the young woman didn't need to hear that a second time. The Knight had made a break for the ship, spinning his staff to create a shield to protect his partner in crime. The Binarians split in half. Some focussed on the duo attempting to abscond, the rest focussed on Brandon.

"This wasn't in the deal!" Brandon shouted, his words drowned by the two ships overhead locked in their own confrontation.

"Stand down!" the Alliance ship said again as it spun in a dance with the Second Chance. "If you do not stand down, we will be forced to shoot you out of the sky!"

With no pilot, the Second Chance couldn't give any verbal response via the speakers. Brandon could have tapped into the communications, but he had his own thing going on.

The bounty hunter scoped the location to try and get a read on where his bounty had gone, and picked out the location of the Knight, who had made it to his ship long before the woman he was protecting could catch up.

Binarians who were on their tail continued to march towards the ship and the people who murdered their royal family, while the Binarians who had turned their attention to Brandon engaged in a light firefight.

Brandon threw gadgets here and there to distract his aggressors. Repulsor orbs to send some flying. Flash grenades to blind. Micro black holes to restrict. Every effort he made was non-lethal.

The same was said for the Second Chance. Despite having weapon systems on board, the autopilot never engaged them. Instead, power went to the shielding and the evasive manoeuvres. The Second Chance and the Alliance ship it faced off with were an even match on those terms, so what resulted was a ballet of non-confrontation.

Over at the Last Knight of Binary's ship, things came to life. The lights across its undercarriage came on, one by one, and the steps for the woman to join Xander lowered for her. Binarians continued to approach the escape attempt, but they were still at some distance. Brandon continued to dodge and dive out of the way of the sudden Binarian aggression, but his eyes were pulled towards the sight of the Last Knight of Binary's immaculate ship.

Moments before it exploded.

The entire ship became many parts of a ship, and the woman the Knight had once escorted was flung by the event. The destructive force of the blast shot her all the way back down the sand dune they had previously crossed, her body bounced and rolled into the distance.

Brandon froze in that moment of shock, and the Alliance ship above even spun to see the commotion, momentarily distracted. A fireball of wreckage and the loss of the Last Knight of Binary. Virgil and the remaining Binarians held their fire, and moved around to look to the aftermath of what they had no-doubt perpetrated themselves.

Which was the perfect moment for Brandon to whistle the Second Chance once again, grab a cube out of his satchel, throw it towards the sand dune, and leap onto his unfolding hoverboard to look for the remains of his bounty.

Chapter Six

The alien woman continued to roll and scatter sand in the air as she tumbled down the sand dune. She didn't make a sound as she fell, no doubt in shock of the sudden massive explosion. Without the Knight by her side, it was down to Brandon to track her down.

Brandon launched off the ridge and down towards the young woman. Smoke rose and debris continued to fall behind him has he withdrew from the conflict with the Binarians and the destruction of the Knight's ship.

It wasn't hard for Brandon to spot his bounty. All things considered in the past few moments, the bounty hunter didn't exactly take kindly to an employer opening fire on him, thus Brandon chose to regroup, and evaluate whether what he was doing was the right thing.

That is, however one can classify the "right thing" in bounty hunting.

All he knew was that there had to be a communication problem between the Binarians and himself. Surely.

He reasoned this to himself as he made it closer to the incapacitated usurper to the throne of Binary.

The body had finally come to a stop at the base of the sand dune. Memtorian sand ingrained the skin that was naturally flecked. Several small cuts seeped green blood, but overall, the woman suffered no serious wounds from the explosion. Brandon looked above him, to the ridge he leapt off, and saw that the Alliance ship still hovered around, but had now turned its attention exclusively on the Binarians.

"Stop where you are!" the bounty hunter could hear the ship say.

Brandon determined that going back that way wasn't wise with the Alliance looming down on them and the Binarians potentially trigger-happy. So he instead opted to carefully pick the woman up and stand her on the back of the hoverboard to whisk her to a safe location.

He struggled a little getting her to stay upright behind him – the hoverboard didn't exactly have cargo options – but once he managed to do so, he draped the bounty's arms over his shoulders, kept her stable, and carefully kicked off to take the two of them away from under the nose of those nearby.

Several miles later, the two of them were a place far away from the dunes of the Memtorian sands and the Alliance-riddled Mobius. It was here when the figure draped against Brandon's back came to.

"Urrrgh…" she muttered. Her eyes went from a slow open to a sudden one. "What?!"

The woman struggled and protested as she got up from her resting position against Brandon. The bounty hunter looked over his shoulder as the hoverboard was moved side to side by the bounty's movements.

"Hey! Hey, wait!" Brandon said, trying to keep the board stable. "If you do that too much you'll be thrown right off here!"

"What's going on?" she said, looking around. Her grip of Brandon only tightened out of fear. "Where are we?"

"We're still on Memtoria, don't you worry about that," Brandon said, slowing the hoverboard down. "But we're…somewhere different."

"Where's Xander?" she spun. "Where's my Knight?"

"He's…well…he's…" Brandon said, his face softened.

"Where?!"

"I last saw him getting into your ship."

"He left without me?"

"S-Something like that…" Brandon said as he brought the board to a standstill and hopped off. The woman followed and the hoverboard began to fold into a cube again.

"He did?!" the woman said. She lowered her gaze. On realisation, she tapped at her face and pulled away, looking at her own blood that escaped from the scrapes on her face. "He did."

Brandon picked up the cube and stashed it away. His hand remained near his holstered Stunderbuss, but he didn't go for it.

"Poor fool probably didn't know what happened," Brandon said. "I've seen that before. Wired explosives to the starter engine. Turn on, blow up."

The woman looked up at the bounty hunter. Her eyes narrowed to slits. Step after step she sped up as she approached Brandon. The usurper's eyelids flicked open as she pulled out a retractable vibro-short sword and swung it at the bounty hunter.

Brandon reacted just in time to parry it with his Stunderbuss and shoot a warning shot past her left ear.

"You killed him!" the woman shouted.

"No! No I didn't!" Brandon said, holding firm. "I don't kill people!"

"You killed a person!" the woman said. "You killed the only person I trusted!"

"I did not!" Brandon said. "I…was about to capture you two until…"

The woman leaned forwards by an inch. "'Capture'?…"

Brandon took a step back. The woman compensated.

"Yes. My name is Brandon Falcon, and I'm a bounty hunter," he explained. "And I was employed by the Steward of Binary to bring both you and your friend back for a fair trial."

"'Fair trial'?" the woman brandished her blade. "They want to kill me!"

"Well, yeah," Brandon admitted. "I guess that's what you get for what you've done."

And without a moment to soak it all in, the bounty hunter whistled once again, which de-cloaked the Second Chance and momentarily distracted the usurper.

Then the bounty hunter pulled the trigger of the Stunderbuss, and brought the woman to the floor.

Brandon sipped at a cup of Coca-Cola from the replicator as he made his way to the holding cells. The ship was already making distance from the planet of Memtoria by the time he was relaxed in the comfort of the Second Chance, checking up on his bounty.

The usurper to the Binarian throne sat in the middle of her cell, eye contact constantly locked on the bounty hunter.

"So…" Brandon sipped at his drink. "What do you think of the Second Chance?"

"Excuse me?" the woman said without a care.

"The Second Chance, my ship!" the bounty hunter took another sip. "It's great, no?"

"No."

"Oh."

The woman sighed and unfolded her legs. She stood up.

"I do not exactly have time to care when I'm being brought to the firing squad that will execute me."

"Well aren't you melodramatic."

"It's true," the woman said. "Well, apart from the firing squad. I will likely be beheaded, knowing them."

"Damn," Brandon swirled his drink. "I guess that's what you get for what you did."

"Which is what, exactly?" the woman moved towards the bars of the holding cell. "What did those spineless scum tell you about what I've done?"

"You know, regicide, mass murder, attempting to seize the throne, all that fairy tale stuff."

The woman gave a blood-curdling chuckle. Despite having the bars between then, Brandon began to wish he had his Stunderbuss on him.

"And instead of an army they send you?" the woman said. She measured him up with a scanning gaze. "A *bounty hunter*."

"Hey, don't knock the profession. I succeeded."

"*Half*-succeeded," she said as she turned and walked over to the bench at the back of the cell. She sat down. "*If* I believed that you didn't rig that explosion yourself."

"It was the Binarians," Brandon said.

"So why didn't you let them kill me there too? Why capture me and delay the inevitable?" the woman wondered aloud.

"Because clearly the deal had changed."

"When?"

"After they started shooting at me."

"Oh?" the woman's mouth formed a grin. "So they didn't have the honour you thought they would have?"

"Lady, I'm a bounty hunter," Brandon relaxed. He wasn't going to let her take control of the situation. "Honour's a hazy concept in my line of work."

"Which would explain why there's a Binary ship on your tail right now," the woman said.

"Huh?" Brandon shrugged and went to sip his drink. As he did, a warning shot clipped the Second Chance's shields, causing the ship to shake, Brandon's cup to miss his mouth, and a stream of Coke to spill down his front.

"Warning!" Cherry said across the ship's speakers. "An unidentified ship has fired on us."

"Yes, Cherry! I noticed!" Brandon shouted.

"And it's a Binary ship," the woman identified.

"How did you know that?" the bounty hunter said.

"I can sense it."

"Really?" Brandon put his cup down and neatened himself up.

"No. There's a window," the woman said. She pointed over Brandon's shoulder.

The bounty hunter followed her finger and looked out into the space beyond the window, and the Binary ship that was tailing the Second Chance.

"Great, just great," Brandon spun towards the corridor and accelerated. "You stay put, Princess. I have a feeling I'm not going to get paid by these guys."

"Oh, so you've been properly informed on who I am then!" the woman shouted after Brandon.

"Huh?" Brandon tapped at the door release on his way towards the bridge.

"I'm the last surviving Princess of Binary," she shouted. "Or I guess now I'm the rightful Queen of it."

"What."

And a second shot rocked the starboard side of the ship.

Chapter Seven

There wasn't time to process what he had heard. The Second Chance was under attack by a Binarian ship, and Brandon had to deal with that first.

The bounty hunter ran down the corridors of the ship, navigating his way to the bridge. His cup of Coke was left somewhere behind him, thrown away in the need to get the ship into evasive action. Cherry was a capable-enough autopilot, but the Second Chance needed Brandon's touch.

"Cherry. Status report!" Brandon requested, slipped into captain mode.

"We are being attacked by one ship. Identified as a Binarian cruiser," Cherry described. Brandon tapped in the access code for the bridge.

"One ship. I can deal with one ship," the captain nodded. He leapt into the pilot's seat and flicked the necessary switches. One by one, lights on the bridge came to life, and Brandon pulled up the ship's control sticks.

A red light flashed on the ship console. A warning sound blared alongside it.

"Warning," Cherry said. "More ships inbound."

"I cannot deal with more than one ship," Brandon frowned. "How much longer until they hit?"

Another shot from the sole Binary ship rocked the Second Chance's shields. From the bridge, the bounty hunter saw the telltale blue flash of the ship's protection flickering under the blow.

"It will be a matter of minutes, Captain," Cherry said.

"Any read on the numbers?"

"At least a dozen with equal or more dangerous firepower."

"Brilliant," Brandon sank in his seat. "Why not tell me some good news."

"As of right now, all systems still remain fully operational."

"Fantastico," Brandon cracked his fingers. "Lets see how that ship does trying to keep us in its sights."

Brandon pushed down on both sticks and took the Second Chance into a dive. He watched as the Binary ship fired a missing shot that flew over the bridge. The bounty hunter smiled and pulled the ship harshly to the right. As his ship went into a roll, Brandon pulled back up. A Grasshopper-Class ship like the Second Chance was perfect in evasive manoeuvres. It had a tight turning sphere that did well for going back on oneself, and with Brandon at the controls and with his experience, the Second Chance effortlessly danced around the skies.

Without a crew, however, the Second Chance couldn't do much more. Cherry could only help things so much. Without a dedicated weapons expert or an engineer the captain's ship couldn't do too much to fight back, let alone escape.

So instead, Brandon had chose the option to stall as he thought about his options.

"Okay, so these Binarians aren't so much going to pay me as they are just going to blow the two of us out of the sky," he pondered. "Which is an outcome I'm not particularly fond of."

"Um, Captain," Cherry said. "The prisoner on board wants to be patched in."

"I'm kinda busy, Cherry!" Brandon shouted, twisting and twirling the Second Chance through the surrounding space.

"Bounty Hunter?" the supposed Princess said over the ship's speakers.

"Yes...*Princess*?" Brandon replied. "I'm kinda busy here!"

"Those people will never negotiate," she replied.

"I gathered!" Brandon struggled, pulling the ship back up.

"They will just gather more numbers. You don't want this war."

"You're right! I don't! Maybe I should just kill you and maybe they'll leave you alone!"

Brandon spun the ship around 180 degrees. He looked upon the ship in front of him. A crescent moon of silver and black. Mirrored to a degree. It fired at the Second Chance, and the shields flickered once again.

"Captain," Cherry said. "Any more hits and the shield will break."

"Don't worry, I've got this," Brandon brushed away. With the delay between shots, we'll recharge enough each time to buy enough time.

"For what, Captain?"

"For..." Brandon began, but he didn't finish.

Because behind the single Binary ship was an approaching formation of ships.

Brandon fell silent and sat up in his seat, looking left to right, counting the number of ships in his head. More than enough to tear the Second Chance into stardust.

"No, I'm not losing my ship," Brandon said. His gauntlets tightened around the controls.

"Whether you surrender or not, Bounty Hunter," the Princess said over the speakers. "We're doomed. You and your ship."

"That's not going to happen," Brandon said, adamant. "We shall just wait."

The bounty hunter did the calculations in his head. The data he had gathered from the evasion of the Binarian ship gave him something to work off. Brandon formed a plan in his head, but it had to be pulled off at the right moment in the right conditions.

One by one, the Binarian ships joined the single ship that was there from the start. Together they formed a constellation of murder and destruction, but it was all for one ship, and one person.

They really wanted that woman dead. And if she was the last surviving Princess of Binary, the story was completely different than what he thought.

"Prisoner," Brandon said into the bridge microphone. "Are you who you say you are? Are you actually a Princess?"

"My late protector and I are bound by different codes, but we both have honour. Unlike those who seek to destroy me," the prisoner spoke softly. "I am indeed Princess to the Kingdom of Binary. And if you continue the work of the great Xander Xerdian in protecting me, I shall see you rewarded."

Brandon tapped his golden fingertips against the ship's console. There wasn't much time left as the Binarian ships regrouped and reformed.

"How?"

"If you can manage to get me back to Binary, and help me re-take the throne as Queen, then you may pick from the many riches of my kingdom."

The Binarian ships began to charge up their weapons. A single concentrated shot from each would combine into a blast that would wipe every single atom of the Second Chance and its contents from existence.

"Already that seems way more risk than reward. Why should I trust you?" a bead of sweat dripped down Brandon's temple.

The door to the bridge lifted open.

"Because I just activated the hyperdrive," said the Princess as she stood at the threshold.

The bounty hunter didn't look behind to see her standing there. He had more pressing things to deal with. Like the imminent destruction of his beloved ship. Which was not going to happen if he had anything to say about it.

So he pulled up on the stick, slammed the big blue button for the hyperdrive, and slingshot the Second Chance over the heads of all the Binarian ships. By the time they managed to turn around, Brandon, the princess, and the Second Chance would be lightyears away, hidden in a direction and location unknown to the aggressors. For the moment, the unlikely duo in the fleeing ship was safe.

But moments later, they were stranded.

"Okay," Brandon finally said after the ship slowed down before it shut most of itself down. "What is going on?"

"I believe," the princess said, "We have stopped."

"I gathered that much."

"You're welcome, by the way."

Brandon reached for a Stunderbuss that he didn't have. He clenched his fists.

"How did you get out of the cell? How did you know how to activate the hyperdrive? How did you even manage to do that without even being in the room?!"

"You ask a lot of questions, Bounty Hunter," the princess said. "You should have asked this many before you decided to commit regicide."

"But *you* committed regicide!"

The princess shook her head and stepped into the bridge. She looked around with a mild look of disgust.

"I did no such thing," the Princess said. "Binarians are a people of honour."

Brandon nodded. "And if I believe you, you're talking about people ready to eradicate their own princess."

The princess shook her head and turned away from the bounty hunter.

"Those are *not* Binarians."

"Then who – "

Brandon stopped talking the moment the lights on the ship went off.

"Ship commencing emergency shut down," Cherry said.

"Wait, what?!" Brandon ran back to his chair and began pressing buttons and flicking switches.

"You overloaded the ship," the Princess muttered.

"The Second Chance suffered an overload due to the sudden stress of activity coupled by using the hyperdrive for too long," Cherry explained. "Ship now operating on minimal power."

Brandon banged his fist on the ship console and tried all manner of things to try and get the ship working again.

"Well take it off minimal power!"

"Ships damaged, it needs replacement parts," the princess muttered once again.

"Negative," Cherry said. "Damage has been caused throughout the engine room. Replacement parts needed."

The bounty hunter raised his head at the echoing of responses and looked back over to the bounty that had brought nothing but trouble. Brandon hopped out of his seat and went straight to the princess.

"How are you doing that? Are you causing that?" Brandon said, eyes focused on her, looking around for any devices.

"You really do have a lot of questions, Hunter," the princess said. "Yet you haven't once asked for my name."

"I'll bite. What's your name?"

"It is Ceres Si'Mina," the princess curtseyed. "The Lost Queen of Binary Fields, as I hear they've begun to call me."

Ceres stepped over and sat in the seat next to Brandon's. The bounty hunter looked around to the princess in confusion.

"Who calls you that?"

"The people of Binary."

"They call you the usurper to the throne."

"Oh. *They* call me that," Ceres shook her head. "But not the people. The *true* people."

"As much as I'm loving playing 20 Questions with you," Brandon said. "I need to get my ship moving again."

"You won't be able to do that," Ceres informed. "With an overloaded, damaged ship on minimal power, there's not much you can do."

"You don't know anything about my ship," Brandon went to leave. "Nobody does, except me."

The bridge door slammed down before Brandon could step through it. He groaned and began to type the code into the panel.

"I know enough," Ceres said.

Before Brandon could finish typing in the access code the door shot back up. The bounty hunter looked over to his unwelcome guest.

"I'm a technopath," Ceres shrugged. She waggled her fingers without much thought. As she turned her attention back to the door, the princess began to lower the bridge door again, little by little.

Despite being on the other side of the room.

"A technopath?" Brandon repeated. He looked to her and to the bridge door. "Huh."

"Yup," Ceres said, and turn her attention to the ships controls.

Brandon raised a hand.

"Whoa," Brandon said. "Don't do anything silly."

"I'm not," Ceres said, eyes locked on the control panel. With a blink, a green light on the console lit up and began blinking. The princess began to speak. "This is the Second Chance broadcasting on all covert channels. Our ship has suffered a malfunction that requires parts we do not have. We are stranded and in need of assistance. The less interference with the Alliance, the better. I repeat. This is the Second Chance in need of assistance. Our co-ordinates are encoded into this recording. Please help. We shall reward you greatly."

"That's the silliest thing you could have done!" Brandon ran back to the console. "You realise you just opened our doors for anyone to come on in?"

"Exactly my plan."

The bounty hunter was angry, but there wasn't anything else he could have done. They were stranded in deep space, and if no-one found them soon, they would be for the rest of their short lives.

Chapter Eight

With most of the ship's systems out of commission, Brandon and Ceres sat across from each other in the common room. The captain hunched over his Lucky Charms while the princess sat awkwardly in front of him.

"So..." Ceres began.

"So we wait," Brandon said, spooning another lot of sugar into his system.

"Do you not have a kitchen?" the princess looked around.

"*No*, the Second Chance does not have a kitchen," the bounty hunter replied. "But we do have a replicator. I'm sorry this isn't a palace, *Princess*."

Ceres tapped her feet against the cold floor of the Second Chance and sighed.

"Replicator: Apples."

Nothing happened. Ceres looked to the bounty hunter in expectation. Brandon lowered his spoon back into the bowl of mostly milk and explained.

"Sure, the technopath can psychically control technology, but the Second Chance's A.I. is still hardcoded to respond to me and only me," he turned to address the ship's A.I. "Replicator: Apples."

Nothing again.

"Captain. Remember what I said. I have a name," the A.I. said.

Brandon groaned. "*Cherry*: Apples. Please."

"'Cherry'?" Ceres mouthed.

"Cherry is the name of the ship's A.I.," Brandon said as he picked his spoon back up. "I programmed her. I designed her."

"You did?" Ceres sat up. "Impressive."

Brandon clicked his fingers and the nearby monitor switched on. *TaleSpin* flashed onto the screen, and the bounty hunter in a short moment began to laugh at the animated antics from centuries gone by.

"Well, you know," Brandon said. "The ship already had A.I., I just did some modifications. Over half of the Second Chance is modifications."

The captain looked up and around his ship in admiration and affection. There was a warm feeling that filled Brandon as he reflected on his home. In his eyes, the bounty hunter melted back to being a kid looking upon a beautiful sight for the first time.

"Do these modifications include the susceptibility to breaking down?" Ceres asked.

"My ship does not break down!" Brandon snapped back. He looked to the pipes that snaked along the walls. "She just hasn't had to go through that much stress in a long…long time."

Brandon thought for a moment, and then began to slurp the rest of the milk in his bowl up. Ceres picked up one of the dozen of apples that the replicator created. She pulled out a small knife and began to cut it.

"You love your ship, don't you?" Ceres said, lifting the slice of apple to her mouth. It crunched under her teeth in perfection.

"Oh, you're a telepath too, I bet," the bounty hunter said.

"I don't need to read your mind to see the truth," Ceres said. "And I can't read minds, so you're fine."

The bounty hunter nodded, and placed his bowl in the disposal.

"Cherry: OJ."

Brandon took his orange juice and turned his attentions back to the TV.

"What…is this?" Ceres commented.

"*TaleSpin*," Brandon said, eyes locked on the cartoon.

"Huh?"

"It's a cartoon," the bounty hunter explained. "Entertainment. From the planet Earth. A few hundred years ago."

"You have recordings from Earth?"

Ceres turned her attentions to the monitor as well. It wasn't before long until she was engaged with the sight.

"Not recordings," Brandon said. A light in his peripheral vision began to blink, momentarily distracting him. "What you're seeing is a live transmission. From all those lightyears away, the Second Chance is only just getting these signals."

"How is that possible?"

"Sometimes, Princess, the Universe has a surprise for you. Whether that be a star that meets a black hole, the creation of another galaxy, or the fact that we can get a live broadcast of *Darkwing Duck* from 250 years into the future."

"What is '*Darkwing Duck*'?"

"My, my, Princess," Brandon reclined. "If we're gonna be stuck here for good, at least you'll be able to experience my favourite cartoon of all of those from Earth before we go."

"Maybe," Ceres said. "Except that looks like someone's responded to our distress beacon."

Brandon sat up and followed Ceres' point towards the other monitors in the room. The bounty hunter smiled and leapt towards the data, excited at the sign of other intelligent life.

"Woohoo!" he grinned. Brandon pressed a few buttons and turned on some dials to communicate to the approaching ship. He watched the blip on the radar move closer to the one that stood for the Second Chance. "Man, I sure am happy you're here! You're a good Samaritan! You're saint! You're…"

"*Falcon*!" a robotic voice buzzed over the speakers.

"…Lenny," Brandon finished.

"It's L3-NY, meatsack!"

"Yeah, yeah, but it sorta looks like Lenny when it's written down, you gearbucket," Brandon muttered. He pressed the button to speak again. "Alright, are you gonna help me out here, or what?"

"Maybe. Are you gonna give me back my leg?"

Brandon cursed under his breath. He pressed the button. "You know I can't do that, Lenny. This ship has enough missing parts as it is right now."

"I was missing a leg!"

"And you got another one, clearly you didn't miss it *that* much!" Brandon punched a few commands into the ship's computer. "Right, I've activated the ship's magnet strips. Lock on, help me fix my ship, and then lets just go our separate ways."

"If you're not gonna address the leg thing, at least let me punch you very hard in the face."

Brandon thought for a second.

"Make it the gut."

"Deal."

"Come on in."

Brandon disconnected the conversation and turned to Ceres.

"Friend of yours?" she asked.

"Urgh," Brandon grimaced and shook his head. "Just don't. Stay put, I'll deal with this."

The bounty hunter walked to the exit, grabbing his revolver on the way. He checked the few bullets that he had, and then put the gun in his waistband. Had to be prepared in case L3-NY didn't keep his word.

And if he attempted to punch Brandon in the face.

Once again L3-NY and Brandon faced each other at the starboard airlock doors. The droid's ship was docked and locked against the Second Chance's magnet strips, and the droid himself waved through the window.

"Not gonna shoot me again, are you?" L3-NY said.

"Nope," Brandon raised his empty hands. "I really need the help. You got parts?"

L3-NY raised a bag. "I've got parts."

The bounty hunter nodded and opened the airlock door. As it came up, the gun in L3-NY's other hand was revealed.

"I also have a gun," L3-NY said. "As insurance."

Brandon lifted his shirt to reveal the butt of his revolver.

"Me too."

"You really do think you're a badass, don't you?" L3-NY's neon eyes flashed.

"Says the bounty hunting bucket of bolts with the paintjob and the fancy new leg."

L3-NY's gun warmed up for a couple of seconds in his anger. It cooled off as he did.

"Just take me to your engine room, meatsack."

"You definitely need more slurs," Brandon said. He gestured over for L3-NY to follow him.

The uneasy alliance continued as the captain and the droid made their way deeper into the heart of the ship. As you got closer to the heart of the Second Chance, the rooms became less civilised and more of a semi-organised mess. More labyrinthine pipes and wires and computing showed their face as the Second Chance revealed the true backbone of the ship that Brandon had built his life on top of.

"You know, I haven't been this deep into a ship in a long time."

"Really? I'm always down here in the down time. When there's nothing on the monitors and bounty hunting's slow and all that, I'm around in the bowels of the ship. Doing modifications. Improvements. Additions."

"Clearly it's a patchwork job," L3-NY said as he looked at the dodgy welding and wiring jobs he could see.

"Well, you know, this isn't exactly my area of expertise. I'm not just a captain here. I have to do everything."

"So do I, Falcon," the droid said. The bag of parts clanged and jingled around with each step. "Then again, I'm not running a Grasshopper."

"It's the Second Chance, Lenny," Brandon corrected. "It's not a Grasshopper Class any more. It's something different. A Brandon Falcon original."

Nearby, a light blew and sparks shot across the corridor.

"Oh yeah, that's so much better."

It wasn't long until they found themselves at the engine room. To be more accurate, the Second Chance had two primary engines a couple smaller ones. The full specifics of how the ship worked were a detail so complex, Brandon himself didn't even know what the full extent of the problem was.

"Errm…" the bounty hunter said as he examined the room. "…There!"

"What, where that small fire is burning?" L3-NY observed.

"Yes!" Brandon skipped over to the fire and stamped it out. He breathed and looked over the damage. Which was a fair amount of it. "It looks like…it's broken."

If L3-NY had the right sockets, he would have rolled his eyes.

"You are so lucky I'm a gracious saviour," the droid said, lowering the bag he had. "What have you even done back here?"

The captain shrugged. "You know…added a few auxilliary engines. Tinkered with the fuel and power supply to give the ship some extra oomph. Re-routed the old communications array to boost its signal. Installed…"

"Wait," L3-NY said, his bag of parts open. The droid looked over Brandon's modifications. "That's…That's…"

"Now's not the time, Lenny," Brandon said. Above him, warning red lights began to flash. "Just help me fix my ship."

"Falcon, you know I'm not doing this out of the goodness of my own heart."

"Course not. You don't have one."

"Cute. I mean, you know I'm doing this because it doesn't seem fair to take you out when you're already down for the count."

"I know you have a grudge, Lenny," Brandon said, concerned over the lights overhead. "But come on. There must be some sort of bounty hunter code you have to adhere to."

"We're bounty hunters! There is no code!" L3-NY said. He pulled out a few parts and began putting them together, combining them with what was left of the damaged ones. "As soon as this ship is up and running, I'll give you the count of 20. Then I don't care about trying to board. I'm shooting you right out the sky."

"You get my ship up and running and that's a deal," Brandon said. He only paid a little attention to the droid. The bounty hunter was too busy wondering what the flashing lights were for.

"Just like old times, ain't it, Falcon?" L3-NY said as he worked.

"Yeah," Brandon mumbled. "Cherry: What's going on?"

"Warning lights engaged."

"Your A.I. doesn't have as much of that 'intelligence' as you'd hope," L3-NY said with a mechanical laugh.

"Says the robot?"

After a few clicks of his tools, L3-NY stood back up.

"I'm a droid."

"What's the difference?"

"You skinballs are so racist."

"Says the robot who just called me a 'skinball'!"

"Droid!"

"Rabbit season!"

"...What?"

Both Brandon and L3-NY snapped out of their confrontation as the red warning lights were then coupled with the sounding of an alarm.

"Oooh, the alarms are back on!" Brandon said. "Why are the alarms back on?"

"I fixed your junkyard of a ship."

"That fast?"

"I'm fast."

"That's alright," Brandon patted L3-NY's cold shoulder. "Most robots suffer performance issues."

The droid punched Brandon's shoulder. Hard.

"Zip it. What's all this noise for?"

"It's alright. I know what's going on," Brandon stepped past L3-NY, nursing his shoulder. "Cherry: ...What's all this noise for?"

Yet again, the droid wished he could roll his eyes.

"Oncoming asteroid storm," Cherry reported.

"See?" Brandon shrugged. "Just an asteroid st-...an asteroid *storm*?!"

L3-NY's eyes shot into a rich neon green. "No no no no!"

And the droid pushed past the bounty hunter and ran back to the starboard doors.

Brandon chased L3-NY through the bowels of his ship. He grinned as the lights all around him began coming on one by one, and laughed in joy as the Second Chance began making all the noises he knew and loved. Everything was fully operational again, and he would thank the droid that helped him fix it, if it wasn't for A) They had a mutual uneasiness and B) The ship began to get pelted by asteroids.

L3-NY's feet echoed throughout the Second Chance's halls as he navigated his way to his exit. There wasn't a moment of hesitation. He knew the lay of the land and never once stopped. L3-NY had a great sense of direction, but even that coupled with speed didn't look to be enough.

Brandon caught up with L3-NY at the starboard airlock door. L3-NY began typing into the access panel to open the door, but was met with incorrect keycode errors.

"This isn't your ship," Brandon said. "Different codes."

The droid banged his fist repeatedly on the door. "Let be back onto my ship! I can't – "

An asteroid collided and the two of them were sent across the room. L3-NY made a clang against the pipes in the room while Brandon made a thud between his head and the ground.

"Ow…" Brandon rubbed his head. He stood up and walked back over to the airlock door.

"Come on, Falcon, I fixed your ship!" L3-NY said. "Now let me back onto mine!"

"Lenny…"

"I'll count to 30! 50!"

"Lenny…" Falcon said. He typed into the access panel.

"I knew you'd do it, meatsack. I…"

L3-NY stood and watched as the magnet strips disengaged and his ship began to float away from the Second Chance.

"*Why* did you do *that* for?!" the droid rushed up to the window. He pressed his sensors to the glass before turning back to Brandon. L3-NY drew his weapon and aimed it at the bounty hunter.

"Whoa, wait," Brandon raised his hands. He pointed. "Look."

L3-NY paused for a second in doubt, then turned back to look at his ship. It rolled in space, and revealed than an asteroid had torn a massive hole through it.

"I...don't have the parts to fix that..." L3-NY said. All joy had left him.

"It's okay. She's at peace now," Brandon said. He approached the droid.

L3-NY faced the bounty hunter again. Disarmed. He lowered his weapon. Brandon went for a hug.

And L3-NY punched him in the gut.

Chapter Nine

"What," L3-NY said.

"Don't you see the resemblance?" Brandon asked.

The bounty hunter and the droid sat in front of a monitor watching the cartoon *He-Man and the Masters of the Universe*. Brandon took gulps of the glass of orange juice in his hand.

"I am not Skeletor," L3-NY said.

"Not with that attitude!" Brandon said.

The droid raised a cup.

"When you've just lost your ship to asteroids, you aren't exactly put in a place to watch whatever it is we're watching."

"It's *He-Man*!" Brandon said. "Lighten up!"

"You owe me a ship, Falcon."

Brandon finished his drink.

"First it was your leg, now it's an entire ship…" Brandon shook his head. "Why are you so greedy?"

L3-NY took his gun and pointed it square in Brandon's face. The bounty hunter crossed his eyes as he looked down the barrel. It hadn't been fired in a while, but it was certainly in a position to change that.

"Maybe I'll just take *your* ship," L3-NY said, his eyebulbs focusing. "Which, by proxy, has my leg in it!"

"That isn't the wisest move, Lenny," Brandon raised his hands. "I've got a bounty on board."

"All the more for L3-NY!" the droid said. "I'll turn in that bounty, I'll find a way to profit from you, and I'll be the richest droid in the System!"

"Robot."

"I'm a droid!" L3-NY's gun lit up.

"I wouldn't do that if I were you," Brandon reasoned.

"What are you two doing?" asked Ceres.

"Who are you?!" L3-NY changed targets. The princess raised her palms.

"Oh you're in trouble now!" Brandon said. "She's a technopath! Get him!"

Nothing.

L3-NY's head turned to Brandon.

"She's a technopath," L3-NY said.

"Doesn't that mean she can throw you across the room?"

"That's telekinesis," L3-NY corrected.

"So…what can she do?"

"I stopped the droid's gun," Ceres said. She didn't make any movements, but she held her focus with L3-NY and his gun.

"*Thank you,*" L3-NY nodded. "See? *She* calls me a droid."

"I hope that means you're not going to shoot me," Ceres said.

"Oh. Don't worry about that," L3-NY said. "I'll only shoot my old friend over here. You I can just turn in and collect your b–…"

And with that, L3-NY froze.

Shut down.

"You can shut him down?" Brandon asked.

"Well, I *am* a technopath," Ceres lowered her hands and stepped into the room.

The bounty hunter pushed down on L3-NY's gun with one finger. As he did, the droid's arms lowered, weapon in hands. Brandon smirked.

"Looks like you've got your uses," Brandon commented.

"Are we just going to leave him like this?"

"You can reactivate him in a second. I just wanna mess with him a little first."

Ceres later brought L3-NY back to the land of the living. To manipulate a simple system like the droid was a task that wasn't too hard or taxing to a technopath like the princess was.

"–ounty," L3-NY finished. He looked around. "Where am I?"

The droid looked up. Or rather, down.

For Brandon had no problem hanging L3-NY upside down and posed like a teapot.

"You're still on my ship, Lenny," the bounty hunter said. He held L3-NY's very own gun at him.

L3-NY calibrated his eyes. "That technopath is really something."

"Yes I am," Ceres moved to him. "We haven't been introduced. Ceres Si'Mina."

L3-NY offered the hand that was a spout a few seconds prior. "L3-NY. The System's greatest bounty hunter."

"Um, I'm a better bounty hunter than you," Brandon offered. "Maybe the best bounty hunter that's a *droid…*"

"It is a pleasure to meet you L3-NY," Ceres shook the droid's hand.

"And what's a beautiful creature like you done to deserve having a bounty put over your head?" L3-NY said. "Let alone having to spend time on this junk."

"Hey, I'm standing right here," Brandon said.

"I'm being nice here," L3-NY muttered to the bounty hunter.

"Why?"

"Because she can switch me off whenever she wanted to!"

"So can I!" Brandon brandished L3-NY's gun.

L3-NY brushed him aside. "Safety's on."

"No it's n–… " Brandon said. He looked at the gun then aimed it at the ceiling and pulled the trigger.

It fired and dislodged the droid from the pipes overhead. L3-NY crashed down in front of the bounty hunter and the princess.

"Ow," L3-NY groaned.

"You can't feel pain!" Brandon said.

"Yeah, but it doesn't hurt to pretend," L3-NY said as he pulled himself up. He made grabby hands for his gun to be returned. Brandon did so, reluctant.

"I'm a princess," Ceres said.

"Huh?" the droid's eyebulbs lit up.

"That's why I had a bounty over my head," Ceres explained.

"A bounty for a princess?" L3-NY said. "If I didn't know we'd just have a repeat of the last half an hour again, I'd raise my gun and demand to collect your bounty."

"Wise move, Lenny," Brandon said.

"But even so…" the droid turned to the bounty hunter. "If you're looking to collect, why is she walking around as if she's free?"

"New deal."

"What is it now?"

"He's going to protect me," Ceres said. Brandon didn't say anything.

"'Protect'?" L3-NY repeated in non-belief.

Brandon paced around, one hand gliding through his hair and beard.

"If he can bring me back to my planet where I can claim my rightful place, I will reward him greatly," Ceres said.

"How much?" L3-NY asked.

"I'm the soul survivor to a planet-wide monarchy."

"So…"

"A lot."

"What's the catch?"

Brandon filled L3-NY in. "At least a squad of Binarians who want to see her and anyone around her dead. And a group of ships."

"That's just a taste of what they have," Ceres said. "They're re-appropriated an entire fleet of ships plus the planet's defence systems including the holo-dome are operational, ready to destroy all incoming hostiles."

"You didn't tell me that bit," Brandon said.

L3-NY didn't need long to say it how it was. "Looks like it's a – "

"Don't say it – "

"Suicide mission."

"Suicide mission. Yeah," Brandon rolled his eyes.

Silence filled the rather present gap that came after processing the new details.

"I…" Ceres broke the air. "I…realise I'm asking much of you."

"You're saying that…" Brandon mused. "These…people…want to kill you and keep the throne for themselves?"

"Yes."

"And what, are they going to release an age of tyranny against an entire kingdom, guarded by a ton of ships, with a planet that's virtually impossible to land on?"

"But if you can just help me get back to the surface, I have faith we can finish the job," Ceres instilled.

"Everything up until that point though…is a suicide mission."

"It's probably even more of a suicide mission on the surface!" L3-NY added.

The room was quiet once again as the three went into their thoughts. All one could hear as the gentle hum of the Second Chance, back to full working capacity thanks to L3-NY's assistance.

"Captain," Cherry, the ship's A.I. spoke over the speakers. "Would you like some tea?"

"I thought you'd never ask."

In the mess, the trio sat. Brandon got Cherry to project an image of Binary in front of them, and sipped his tea, lost in his thinking. L3-NY cleaned his gun as he looked over the rotating projection, eyebeams focused as they did calculations. Ceres at awkwardly, clutching some tea in her palms, warming her cold skin.

Brandon slurped the last inch or so of his drink, which made the loudest of the few sounds heard by the three of them. Eventually, he finished his tea, and put down the mug with a clatter against the nearby table.

"Okay," he said. "I'm in."

"You are?" Ceres asked. It may have been the tea or the slice of hope that had been presented to her, but one way or another colour came back her paling face.

"But only if you're on board," Brandon nodded, and then he turned to L3-NY. "And if he's on board."

"Me?!" L3-NY protested.

"You don't have a ship, L3-NY," Brandon said. "And I could use someone to control the Second Chance's weapons systems."

"Can't Cherry…"

"I need you behind the controls."

"Surely Ceres…"

"L3-NY," Brandon said. "If there's any hope saving the princess and a planet and getting a score bigger than anything you've ever gotten before, it's with you by our side."

"I don't think…"

"The advance on my original bounty was 1,111,111 Credits. You can have it."

"I think I'm in."

"But that advance you got was…" Ceres interjected.

"Shhh!" Brandon hushed.

L3-NY looked to the bounty hunter and to the princess and to the projection and sighed. He holstered his gun and sat back in his seat.

Brandon stood up in front of the droid and the princess and put his hands on his hips. He nodded, and he sighed, and he waved his hand to disperse the projection of Binary. Brandon picked up his cup and disposed of it and scratched his bearded chin.

"We're not ready."

"What?" Ceres stood up. "You just said you were in!"

"At the moment it's just the three of us against the Binarians."

"They're not Binarians."

"Whoever they are, there's too many of them," Brandon said. "We need time, we need a plan, we need help."

"But they'll catch up with us, Brandon," Ceres said. "If we don't go to them, they'll overrun us and I'll end up like my father. My mother. My aunts. Uncles. Cousins. My little brother."

Brandon turned his back to the princess and walked towards the door.

"I'm setting a course back to Aurora," Brandon said over his shoulder.

L3-NY stood up.

"Hey, wait, whoa, Aurora?" he asked. "Can…can we not?" he awkwardly laughed. "I sorta have…unfinished business back there I'd much rather not close a deal on."

"We all have unfinished business, L3-NY," Brandon said as he typed into the access panel. "Stow it. We're heading back."

"You *hate* those Alliance meatsacks. Even more than I do!"

"We need help," Brandon stepped through the opened doorway. "But I'm not asking the Alliance."

"Falcon!" L3-NY shouted to a bounty hunter that was already halfway towards the bridge. "Urgh, you're gonna get us all killed."

"I trust him," Ceres said, eyes cast towards where Brandon was.

"Don't do that," the droid said. "Last time *we* did, I ended up floating in deep space for months waiting for a ship to salvage me, Brandon ended up losing most of his crew, and Cherry here ended up as this heap of junk's artificial intelligence."

"What?" Ceres moved her attention to the droid's words.

"Cherry," L3-NY commanded. The ship's A.I. responded to his voice. "Playback ship black box recording from Stardate 2266.109."

"Affirmative, Lieutenant Commander L3-NY."

"I'm not a lieutenant commander anymore, Lieutenant Commander Falcon," the droid shook his head.

"Neither am I," Cherry replied. "Playing recording."

Stardate 2266.109

13 years ago, the Second Chance looked a lot different. For one thing, it wasn't the patchwork job that L3-NY was keen on commenting on in the present. 13 years prior, the Second Chance was just a standard-issue Grasshopper-Class vehicle of the Alliance. It was painted regulation blue and silver and was devoid of any post-market modifications.

It was not Brandon's ship. It was the Alliance's.

But Brandon had recently discovered that wasn't a great arrangement.

Captain Brandon Falcon of the Alliance ship Grasshopper-1135 kept his small crew in order: Lieutenant Spike Gagavian, chief engineer; Lieutenant Commander L3-NY, security officer; and Lieutenant Commander Cherry Falcon, science officer and second-in-command on her brother's ship.

"Captain?" Cherry asked the captain as he piloted the Grasshopper. "Are you sure you want to do this?"

"Cherry, it's amazing how my eyes have only just been opened to the Alliance," Brandon said, easing the ship through space. "How they are bent on creating a galactic empire, regardless of what the involved planets want, and that there's this resistance out there, ready to do the right thing, and bring down the Alliance once and for all."

"I told you we needed to tinker with the ship's receiving frequencies," L3-NY leaned towards Cherry. "You pick up recordings of entertainment from the Earth that used to be and all of a sudden we're being forced to join the rebels just in like the movies."

"L3-NY I'm not forcing anyone to do anything, here," Brandon brushed off. "But if you want to leave this ship and re-join an organisation with the intent of Galactic Domination, well, consider yourself dead to me."

"Captain, I would never betray you," L3-NY said. "It's not in my programming. But it is to second guess bad ideas."

"Good thing Cherry got rid of the code that would make you try to sabotage any move against the Alliance, because that would have made things quite impractical."

"Why?" the droid asked.

A split second before a missile hit rocked the ship.

"Because we've just joined the Battle for Aurora."

The Battle for Aurora was a harsh battle between the Alliance and the rebels high above the eponymous planet. An Alliance fleet riddled by hijackings and defectors that tore their numbers down faced off against the accumulated "freedom fighters" from across the System. The captain's ship was one of those defectors who came near the end of the Civil War, a time by which Brandon and his crew had already seen their fair share of bloodshed and destruction.

High above Aurora, the biggest slaughter in the history of the System continued for days, with each side gathering reinforcements each time the opposition thought they had gained the higher ground.

In any other situation, it would be a stalemate. But with the rebels fighting a losing battle throughout the System and with the Alliance still present in a lot of the galaxy in a big way, it was more a delaying of extinction.

Aurora was the key, however. The odds were against the gathered rebels, but if they took Aurora, then maybe they would start a revolution via domino effect.

As Grasshopper-1135 flew into the battle as part of the next wave of reinforcements this notion seemed to be the main plan. The rebels had the upper hand in that moment, and Brandon's ship alongside many repurposed Alliance ships and defector Alliance ships hit at the most critical time.

And damn, the Alliance forces were pushed back.

Green bolts and blue beams and rockets and lasers flew and scattered and bombarded opposing ships. The northwest rebels against the southeast Alliance. Squads flew and chased, smaller ships moved to flank, larger ships steamrolled ahead.

Silence held across the vacuum of space above the bustling planet below. With the advances in technology and the sheer manpower on Aurora, it did not take long to rebuild, but throughout the Battle of Aurora the surface was just deemed a spaceship graveyard. Whatever parts of the destroyed spaceships that didn't burn up in the atmosphere in re-entry crashed down on the metropolises and subsequently destroyed huge chunks of those.

"My god…" Brandon observed, as they broke left as the Alliance brought another volley of fire down upon the rebel forces.

The ship's shields took quite a beating as Alliance ships of all classes concentrated their fire on the incoming reinforcements. The rebels were dedicated, but by this point in the battle, predictable. There were few places for the forces to enter via hyperspace, so the Alliance already had those danger areas covered by Jaguar-Class ships.

"We've flown right into a trap!" Lieutenant Spike called.

"No, just the crossfire of the Alliance's best ships," Brandon said.

"Isn't the Grasshopper-Class one of the Alliance's best?"

"Yes she is," Brandon smirked.

With his crew behind him, operating all the vital areas of the Grasshopper-1135, Brandon had no qualm with dancing the ship around the incoming fire. It was a thing of beauty to have a fully operational Alliance ship. Their politics may not be the best, but they sure made the best ships, Brandon always thought.

He backed up his theory. The captain behind the controls of the Grasshopper-Class ship made a force to be reckoned with. L3-NY was equally talented with his operating of the weapon systems. It certainly helped that he was a droid that shared a lot of code with the control interface, essentially being an extension of the ships weapons capabilities.

But with a mouth.

"You want me to shoot these suckers out of the sky, cap?" L3-NY asked.

"Only shoot them enough to retreat, L3-NY," Brandon maintained. "They may be Alliance, but some of those soldiers are still our friends."

"Friends?" Lieutenant Commander Cherry said. "Do you not see what is going on right now? They don't care who we are, why should we care about them?"

"Lieutenant Commander, we're better than them, and we're better than indiscriminately killing," Brandon said, beads of sweat dripping down his face.

"I have a name, *Captain*," Cherry rolled her eyes.

"I know, Cherry," Brandon said.

"Thank you, Captain."

"I have a name too, Cherry," Brandon smirked.

"Oh yeah, sorry, *Fartbag*."

Brandon couldn't help but laugh at his sister's taunting, but he quickly quietened as the ship's engines stopped spinning.

"Uh-oh…"

"Ships engines are out!" Lieutenant Spike shouted. "Looks like they hit us with a Worm!"

"Well get it out of the system!" Brandon barked.

The engineer typed rapidly into the ship's computer as he searched for a way to stop the restriction.

Meanwhile, the Alliance continued to pelt rebel forces with their increasing firepower. Brandon frantically looked all around to see various rebels being shot out of the sky.

"This is not good, this is not good," Cherry observed. She began pulling levers and turning dials on her controls. "Diverting all power to shields."

"That's not going to help us!" L3-NY barked. "Don't take power away from the weapons! I need those to fight back!"

"Let her do what she does best, L3-NY!" Brandon ordered.

"But Captain! Let me do my–"

"L3-NY that's an order! You are not getting us killed so you can just shoot more Alliance out of the sky!"

Brandon looked out to see the shield flicker repeatedly with each incoming blast. The shield held with more and more of the power being diverted to it, but he was uncertain how much longer they were going to hold.

Lights in the bridge began to dim. All other rooms in the ship had already been sapped of their power. Cherry gave the shields everything they've got.

"Hyperdrive is down, I can't get it back anytime soon!" Lieutenant Spike shouted.

"Do what you can, Spike," Brandon said. "Do anything you can. Just get us out of here."

The captain looked above to see a bombing run of rebel ships. He smiled and watched them speed overhead towards the slow-moving Elephant-Class ships the Alliance hard.

Then his face fell as two-thirds were eradicated by the forces escorting the heavy-duty Alliance ships. Some rebels took suicide runs and flew straight into the bridges of the larger ships, and to some degree, it worked. But for the most part, the rebels were getting wiped off the slate.

Brandon pressed the button to broadcast.

"This is the Grasshopper-1135 requesting assistance. We're sitting ducks here."

"Reinforcements won't be there for another 20 minutes," a voice called.

"Who's this? Is that the Admiral?"

"It's the Alliance, son, we're coming. You're gonna be safe."

"Oh, well, we're…not Alliance any more, Sir," Brandon said.

There was a beat of silence.

"Well, son," the voice said. "May God have mercy on your souls."

The line went dead.

"Well," Brandon melted back into his seat. "That is definitely not good."

The captain sat back at the dead controls of his ship and looked as sea of the Alliance ships parted to reveal a Cyclops-Class.

The Royal Flush of the Alliance fleet.

And it was ready to bombard the remains of what was once Brandon's fellow squad of rebels.

"Captain, I can get the engines working again!" Lieutenant Spike yelled. He unclasped his seatbelt and rushed to the door. "I have to do it manually, there's no power to do it from here!"

"I need the power!" Cherry shouted. Her face was drenched in sweat and tears. Her hands were a blur as they worked to divert every single drop of power into what was remaining of the ship's shields. Even the communications array was down. The artificial intelligence was shut off. The Grasshopper had become a metal coffin for four former Alliance soldiers with a joke of a force field around it.

"Come on, give me something!" L3-NY said. "Let me at least take a few down in a blaze of glory!"

"L3-NY, no!" Brandon yelled as Spike rushed past. "Spike, no! Don't!"

The ship's shields finally gave way. The Grasshopper-1135 was rattled, bombarded, riddled. Brandon watched as Lieutenant Spike stepped out of the bridge and into an explosion that consumed him. The captain tried futilely to change the ship's course with no power. More shots struck the ship.

The bridge wobbled. Shook. Split.

"Deploy helmets!" Brandon commanded, and hit the button on his chest to deploy the protective bubble around his head. Cherry did the same. L3-NY didn't have to. Cherry and Brandon looked to each other before a hole pierced through the bridge, pulling the captain's sister into deep space.

She screamed, for a moment.

Then she was never to be seen again.

Brandon and L3-NY remained in the ship, alone, but together. For the last 17 seconds. They shared a look, and a nod, and Brandon watched his weapons expert and final remaining friend explode into multiple pieces before being sucked out into space.

And then the captain was alone.

The captain of a sinking ship.

Sinking down the atmosphere towards the planet of Aurora.

And that was the end of the recording.

Chapter Ten

13 years later and once again silence fell in the Grasshopper-Class ship. Ceres couldn't believe the tale that unfolded before her, but L3-NY just shrugged.

"And that's what happens when you stick up for the little guy."

"You and Brandon used to work together back then?"

"Brandon and I used to be *friends*," L3-NY said. "Crewmates. Brothers in arms. But obviously…that was a long time ago."

"How did you even survive?"

"Well it's easy being who I am," L3-NY gestured to his metallic body. "It's hardly challenging to find a way to put me back together. Even if there have to be a few…changes."

Only then did Ceres notice how L3-NY, like the Second Chance, was essentially a patchwork job of technology. His factory model blended with old relics and fresh out-of-the-box parts.

"But I still won't forget how Falcon stole my new leg once upon a time," the droid said as Ceres stared at the legs he had.

The princess looked back up to the droid.

"You and Brandon. Survivors."

"Not that the world that followed was worth living in," L3-NY said as he paced.

Ceres looked to a nearby window. The Second Chance was gliding through deep space on its new course. She had never fathomed being so far away from home, not to mention the notion of visiting so many distant worlds while those she wanted to employ worked on their quest.

"The System sure is beautiful though," Ceres said. "All things considered."

"All things considered," L3-NY repeated. If he could, he would have spat. "I've been blown up and shot at constantly since the Civil War. Sure, I was a bounty hunter, so that sort of makes sense, and yeah, it can be fun, but part of me still wishes for some peace and quiet ever since that day above Aurora. A retirement."

"Then why don't you turn it all in?"

"If Falcon is right about you and you're right about who you say you are, Princess, then I think this bounty might just be the key to following through on that wish."

"You help me, L3-NY, and I promise you can rest."

L3-NY synthesised a sigh.

"Yeah, yeah," he paused. "How about Falcon, what's he getting out of this?"

Metallic tapping came from the doorway.

"Evidently, a history lesson," Brandon said, his gauntleted fingers rolling against the entrance of the room.

L3-NY stood up straight.

"Oh give it a break, Lenny," the bounty hunter brushed away. "It's been forever since the Alliance and the war."

After things held quiet, Ceres spoke up. "Has it?"

The captain looked over to the princess.

"Lenny had no right digging up the past."

"Captain, I just wanted to have full disclosure with the prin– "

"I am not your commanding officer anymore, L3-NY, you don't have to address me like tha– "

"You're right, Falcon, I don't," L3-NY agreed. "But I just thought that if we're going to be working together then – "

"We're bounty hunters now, L3-NY, we arrest people, we kill people – "

"You don't kill people."

"That's right, because I've already lost enough people because of my actions!" Brandon shouted.

L3-NY went quiet.

"And I'm not going to be responsible for any more."

"How do you expect to earn this bounty if you don't?"

"I am not going to kill anyone."

"Is that a promise you can keep, Falcon?"

"If anyone deserves to die here, it's me, so shut the hell up, L3-NY, and let's just get this job done and then go our separate ways once again!"

The droid said nothing more. He locked eyes with his once-captain, and bowed his head. Then he left. Anger stewed in the captain, but he forced it below the surface.

Ceres looked at Brandon. She really looked at him. With the new information passed to her, she reassessed the person she thought was before her. A broken former Captain in the Alliance, whose former crew he all but lost entirely. The death of his chief engineer. The destruction, then later salvage and reconstruction of his security officer. And the fact that

"You made your sister into the A.I. of the ship?"

Brandon opened his mouth to speak, but the words followed beats later.

"It's not her," his voice cracked. "It's a close approximation of her, but it's not my sister. She's gone.

"Cherry," Brandon clearly vocalised for the ship's A.I. "System information."

"I am the artificial intelligence for the ship, The Second Chance. Version 2.473," Cherry said, monotone. "I am built on the UniOS infrastructure, but the majority of my programming is aftermarket modification. My voice is synthesised by samples generated from the ship computer of Grasshopper-1135, and my personality has been generated by a survey from the Second Chance's Captain, Brandon Falcon."

"Are you my sister, Cherry?" Brandon managed to say.

"No, Captain," Cherry replied. "That would be physically impossible."

"Of course it would be," Brandon looked to the ground.

Ceres had the notion to go over and hug the captain and support him, but she did not capitalise on the idea. If anything, she knew Brandon would more likely require space.

The princess quietly turned her back and left Brandon to be by himself. Like he seemed to be a lot of the time.

Brandon trudged back to the bridge to be alone in his thoughts. The bounty hunter had many realities and moments in his personal history to run away from, but he hadn't expected that the biggest score in his career would bring to light all of his downfalls.

In theory, the job would be challenging, but doable with the right preparation. He already had a fellow bounty hunter who had certain skills being a droid and the princess to the planet they needed to storm that also happened to be a technopath, but he needed a little more help.

A few more additions to the Second Chance's crew.

To him, that's all he needed. To have his head in the game, and all the right pieces on the board.

Now, however, he was left with the journey towards picking up the remaining pieces, while 13 years worth of repressed trauma threatened to flare back up.

It may not have been the wisest idea to try and get L3-NY in on the job, Brandon thought. He should have burnt that bridge as soon as the Grasshopper-1135 crashed.

Instead, his former crewmember turned rival turned kinda-sorta crewmember was somewhere on his ship.

"Cherry, give me a position on L3-NY," Brandon said.

"L3-NY is currently inspecting the weapons systems."

L3-NY was certainly the best option Brandon could see on short notice, all things considered. He already knew how the Second Chance operated, plus he was already essentially stranded on-board while events kicked off. The droid was also expendable, in a way, since he could never be completely destroyed. Just so long as his head could be salvaged. Even in deep space. With a head built of the material black boxes are made out of, it's a wonder why he wasn't entirely built of the stuff.

Doubts filled the bounty hunter's head, but he tried his best to flush them out. He began to play Saturday morning cartoons in his head to try and distract himself. He then began to actually play Saturday morning cartoons on the ship's computer to distract himself. It only did so much.

So he made the choice to expedite the journey to Aurora, and flipped open access to the hyperdrive button. The captain put his finger on the button to broadcast his voice throughout the ship.

"Errm, I think you guys should strap yourselves in right about now. Or at least stop standing up," Brandon spoke into the nearby microphone. "I'm going to engage the hyperdrive in T-minus…now."

And he pressed the hyperdrive button.

The experience of hyperdrive is pretty much the sensation of being loaded into a gigantic slingshot. All forward movement is momentarily halted, and instead, one is given the idea of being yanked backwards, tightly into their seat or harshly against the walls and floor behind them. After a handful of seconds of that feeling, that force is released, and the feeling of everything that exists behind the ship's inhabitants escalates to the point where one could believe those objects were just about to shove right through their body as they pushed their way back through space at an extremely-accelerated pace.

Whether those feelings had any actual weight or reality to them is a completely different story, for faster than light travel is a concept in an execution well beyond the processing of minds like the two bounty hunters and a princess of the Second Chance. To them, it was travelling from Point A to Point B in a way that was a couple rungs below teleportation and comfort.

Cherry, the ship's A.I., was most certainly not a human nor a droid that dealt in any physical relation to hyperspeed, and thusly was the perfect processor of information to ensure the safety of the Second Chance and its crew while the hyperdrive was active. Brandon could still engage and disengage the hyperdrive at will, but there was always a chance that something could happen that he could not foresee but Cherry could.

Collisions while in hyperspeed for example. A rarity, but it happens. Ships merging with other ships, ships making violent contact with planets.

Or the near aversion of the Second Chance obliterating itself against a passing prison convoy and the asteroid it trailed behind.

In other words, their unexpected next stop.

Chapter Eleven

Prison convoys in the System were not a rarity given the penchant for crime and general insubordination against the Alliance. Throughout the galaxy there were countless convoys shipping the next batch of prisoners to the next required labour site for the Alliance's benefit.

The one that the Second Chance almost became a little too close to was trailing behind the asteroid 624-VL, a mining mission for resources the Alliance could later use for whatever power they wanted. Energy or otherwise.

Despite the commonality of passing prison convoys in the System, the odds of a ship in hyperspeed colliding with one were still quite low.

"Well, this is far from good," Brandon noted as Cherry brought them back to a cruise.

The bridge door opened and Ceres pulled herself in.

"What do you think you're doing?! At least give us a little more warning before you decide to engage the hyperdrive!"

"I think we've got more pressing issues than that," the bounty hunter said, his eyes still trained on the sight outside.

Ceres followed his eyes and was startled to see the asteroid and the trail of ships behind it.

"What is that?!"

"They're mining," Brandon said. "The Second Chance would have collided with them if Cherry didn't pull us out of hyperspeed."

"That still doesn't answer why you put us in there in the first place."

"Well it wasn't so we could meet these guys, I can tell you that," Brandon leaned forward and began to mutter. "That's…That's a lot of Alliance ships…"

Brandon began to flick switches on the control panel. He shook his head and his eyes darted around the convoy.

"Well, what are we gonna do? Just fly around?"

A light began to flash on the dashboard. Brandon stared at it for a beat before closing his eyes. He shook his head.

"No…they've spotted us."

Fear struck Ceres quite sharply. Having recently been exposed to the history between Brandon and the Alliance, it was only a matter of time until the Second Chance was shot out of the sky. Again.

"What now?! Do we run? Use the hyperdrive again?"

Brandon didn't seem to go for those ideas. "Need to lay off the hyperdrive for a while, we can't overstress it again, it was a pain getting it sorted last time."

L3-NY chimed in from an intercom. "I see a little too much Alliance for my liking, Falcon. Want me to engage the weapons systems?"

Brandon pressed a button to reply to the trigger-happy droid. "That would be super suicide against this workforce. They might just be a prison train, but they have some mighty powerful weapons they aren't afraid to use on convicts attempting escape."

"So?...What's the plan?" Ceres said. The princess paced a little, unsure on what they could even do in the situation presented to them.

"We say hello," Brandon offered. He pressed the button next to the flashing light to engage the communications channel and spoke. "Hello?"

A static voice blared across the bridge's speakers. "Oh thank god! You made it!"

"Excuse me?"

"One ship?! They sent one ship?!"

"I'm sorry, who am I speaking to?" Brandon said, confused.

"Jenkins, sir. I was beginning to wonder if anyone was going to get here on time, but I guess you guys made it."

Brandon tried to wrap his head around things. "Don't worry, Jenkins. We've got this situation under control."

"Are you sure?" Jenkins' voice said, a note of worry. "Because our men have tried to contain the situation, but frankly, we're screwed."

"Just point me in the direction you need me."

"You see that Eagle-Class ship?" Jenkins voice crackled.

Brandon scanned the line-up of Alliance ships and spotted the large transport trailing behind the majority of the convoy. "Gotcha."

"There. Go there. And hurry up."

With a beep and a crack, Jenkins' voice left the ship.

Brandon mulled things over and began to plan in his head silently for a few moments. Ceres stood uneasy before she took a seat next to the plotting bounty hunter.

"So now...we're...helping them?..." Ceres asked.

Brandon didn't say anything in response to that. Instead, he stood up and pressed the button to talk to L3-NY.

"Lenny, get tooled up, we're heading aboard."

"Aboard what?" L3-NY asked.

"There's an Eagle-Class transport ship that needs our help."

"You're want *us* to get on a Alliance ship?!"
"Yeah, isn't that a little stupid?" Ceres added.
"Believe me, it's the only way I can think of getting past this little obstacle without the Alliance blowing us to pieces."
Ceres couldn't believe what she was hearing. "Wait, excuse me, aren't the Alliance very, very bad? Aren't they the very people you wanted to *rebel* from?"
Brandon let out a smirk to try and sway Ceres. "The Alliance are the worst," he said. "So I guess if we do a little sabotage over there it wouldn't be a bad thing."

It didn't take long for Brandon to manoeuver the Second Chance in place to dock with the Eagle-Class ship. After that, all what was needed was for the bounty hunter and the princess to suit up in Alliance uniforms Brandon bought on the black market, ready for infiltration.
Brandon, Ceres, and L3-NY stood at the port doors, ready to board.
"So, we all know the plan?" Brandon asked, as he holstered his Stunderbuss.
"We get on board, we find out what the Alliance want us to do, we help them out…and we do a little something to help ourselves," Ceres nodded.
"Good," Brandon said. He tried not to smirk too much.
"You're just loving this, aren't you?" L3-NY said.
Brandon stepped ahead of the droid and the princess, and put his hand over the button to open the doors.
"Maybe a little."
"Try not to get us killed," Ceres said. "You still haven't helped me out yet."
"We'll get to that, princess," Brandon said. "But first, we've got to get the heck away from these guys."
He slammed his down on the button and the Second Chance opened its doors to the Alliance ship.
"And to do that…We're gonna have to go right into the heart of this ship."

The trio stepped foot on the Eagle-Class transport, and it looked eerily similar to the Second Chance's interior. Shinier and more professional, of course, but Brandon had forgotten his ship's DNA shares that of the prison transport they had entered.
Except in that moment the Second Chance wasn't on fire.

Pandemonium was the word for the Eagle-Class ship, and it was of no wonder why the Alliance on board needed assistance. A lot more than one ship's worth of assistance. Unfortunately, all they had was a bounty hunter, a droid, and a princess. And one of those wasn't the dab hand with a weapon.

An Alliance officer with panic about his face and screaming from the eyes quickly ran up to the trio.

"Jenkins!" Brandon recognised the Alliance officer from a mile away.

"Thank god! You're aboard! Yes...Yes, this way!" Jenkins ushered the three deceptive strangers deeper aboard the ship.

"What's going on?" Ceres asked, looking around the corridors of the ship.

"It's all going to hell, we're done for!" Jenkins said.

"The ship's gonna crash?" Brandon asked.

"Worse, there's a riot!"

"Riot, huh?" the aperture around L3-NY's eyebulbs narrowed.

They went around a corner that led to a walkway overlooking the main hold of the ship.

And sure enough, they could see their riot.

It didn't take a genius to notice that every prisoner had escaped from their cells, not to mention the severe lack of Alliance enforcers to try and keep the situation under control. This was down to the fact that a huge percentage at that time were scattered around the floor, incapacitated.

"Looks like we don't have to do much sabotaging," L3-NY muttered in Brandon's ear.

Brandon tried his best to stay in character. "Well I sure know why you needed us."

"Now do you see why we need more than one ship?!" Jenkins waved his hands wildly.

"Don't worry, sir," Ceres said. "You have the three of us."

"And we'll solve this little problem for you," L3-NY added.

Brandon nodded and then peered over the screaming and the punching and the spontaneous fires below.

"Right. Ceres, you double back and handle any fires and assist any other Alliance towards the rear of the ship," Brandon pointed. Ceres nodded and followed her instructions. "L3-NY, you head to the front of the ship and make sure none of the convicts make their way to the bridge."

L3-NY nodded. "Affirmative, *Captain*," he said, making an effort not to sound *too* sarcastic.

Jenkins turned to look at Brandon. "And me?"

"Take a step to the right," Brandon answered.

The Alliance officer followed the direction with a puzzled expression on his face. "Why?"

After that question was asked, it was answered by the sprinting convict colliding with the officer, taking him out of commission while only temporarily slowing down the recently-freed prisoner.

"That would be why," Brandon said as he took out his Stunderbuss.

With Ceres and L3-NY already sprinting off in different directions, Brandon was free to hold the fort. At least long enough to stop the nearby convict from taking his head off.

Brandon aimed his gun towards the mass of alien standing up from the crumpled heap of Jenkins, but before a shot could be fired, a yellow arm swiped the gun away from him.

"Hey – " Brandon managed to say before the yellow fist on the end of another arm punched his face.

The bounty hunter was flung several feet behind him, the metal wall roughly cushioning his collision. Brandon stepped groggily back onto his feet into a fighting stance, and he took the time to check his nose. Not broken, but a little bloody.

"Okay, ow. I'd say I deserved that, but I didn't."

He looked over to the convict that had delivered the first blow and realised it was a Selenian. A very angry Selenian. Not the best welcoming party to have on an already dystopian prison ship.

"Wait…you look familiar." Brandon waggled a finger. "Have we met?"

"*Falcon…*" the Selenian said. "Because of you, they put me *here*!"

"Well, I *am* a pretty good bounty hunter," Brandon admitted. "I probably put a fair few of you here. Which now I realise means coming aboard here was a bad choice."

He looked back at the other convicts below trying to formulate an escape and succeeding at breaking more Alliance officers' faces.

"Haven't brought in many Selenians recently…" Brandon stroked his beard. "Oh snap, wait, Ko – "

Another sentence was interrupted, this time by the Selenian tackling Brandon against the wall, pinning him a few feet from the ground.

"Ko'Tex?!" Brandon struggled to say under the arm pinning his neck. "Wow, what are the chances?!"

Ko'Tex snarled and flicked open the claw on his other hand. Without warning, the Selenian swished his hand and stabbed it towards Brandon's face, but the bounty hunter was fast enough to deploy his helmet, which narrowly deflected the blow.

"Still haven't learned about my indestructible helmet, I see," Brandon grinned.

Ko'Tex hissed and looked at the Alliance uniform Brandon had on.

"I *knew* you were a Alliance dog."

Brandon's grin fell.

"I told you, I'm not a Alliance dog."

Ko'Tex slashed his claw across Brandon's cheap disguise and tore it open. With a flick of an elbow, Brandon quick-drew his revolver and took at shot at Ko'Tex's arm.

The Selenian groaned and relinquished his grip on the bounty hunter for a second, which was all he needed. Brandon reached for a repulsor orb that in turn flung Ko'Tex across to the other side of the ship, giving some more breathing room.

"Oh Ko'Tex, come on, this fight's just a little too familiar," Brandon taunted.

The lights above him flickered. The plan had begun.

"Well, how about this?" Ko'Tex said, drawing Brandon's attention.

The Selenian gestured at the Stunderbuss he had raised in his hands. The repulsor orb had not only flung Ko'Tex away from Brandon, but the bounty hunter's Stunderbuss as well.

Brandon countered as soon as he could by drawing his Electro-Whip and unfurling it with a crack of his wrist. The electrified wire sent its way towards Brandon's Stunderbuss and coiled around it, giving Ko'Tex a much-needed shock.

It wasn't enough for the Selenian, who still managed to get a shot off before being temporarily thrown. The Stunderbuss blow connected with Brandon's right gauntlet, causing it to spasm, but thankfully for the bounty hunter, it was far from a critical hit.

The bounty hunter pulled on the Electro-Whip and managed to yank the gun away from the Selenian's claws, but only did as much as scatter it halfway between the two locked in duel. Brandon raised his revolver once again, ready to shoot, but chose not to.

All across the room, the lights completely went out as opposed to just flickering, and by the time they came back on, Ko'Tex found himself on an empty walkway, with Brandon gone and his Stunderbuss gone with him.

And the Selenian also found himself face down on the ground.

Brandon sprinted through the corridors of the Eagle-Class ship, tearing away the tatters of his now ruined Alliance uniform. Alliance officers screaming and firing echoed through the halls left and right, while prisoners cheered and jeered. Wires flickered and flashed with the bolts of stray electricity from damaged technology, fires erupted and extinguished under automatic fire extinguishing controls. The yellow and red lights of warning and danger illuminated all of the paths leading from the hold.

But the path Brandon chose was the one carved from L3-NY's trail of humanoid breadcrumbs.

"Let's see how Lenny's doing," Brandon muttered as he tiptoed over Alliance officer and prisoner alike.

Navigating the labyrinthine interior of the Eagle-Class ship, Brandon eventually made his way through all of the carnage that just seemed to continue the closer and closer he got to the bridge.

The bounty hunter took great care to avoid as much future conflict as he could. L3-NY had did his fair share of face-punching by the looks of things, but as Brandon found his route back to the droid, he couldn't help but notice that there were still a lot of convicts on the loose and not that many Alliance officers.

It wasn't before long until his found his way at the doors to the bridge. The bounty hunter knocked with a metallic clang and called out to his robotic ally. "Lenny! Let me in!"

Silence. For a moment.

"Do the secret knock!"

Brandon rolled his eyes. "We didn't come up with a secret knock!"

"Yeah we did! It went like this!"

From the other side of the door Brandon heard L3-NY knock once.

And that was it.

"Seriously?"

Brandon aimed to the right of the door and shot the access panel. It didn't open.

"Did you just try shooting the door open?" L3-NY asked from the other side of the door.

"...Yeah."

"Why do people think that works?" the droid said, and a second later the door opened to reveal L3-NY, the bridge, and the handful of Alliance officers L3-NY had to knock out to gain full access of the bridge.

Brandon followed the droid into the room and looked around. Not a single shot was fired. L3-NY was *good.*

"So, what's the situation?" Brandon asked.

"Well, you know," L3-NY tried not to brag as he put his hands into non-existent pockets. "Took out a fair few escaped prisoners, a lot more Alliance, hacked my way into the bridge, and then brought down everyone you see here. Non-lethally, of course…"

"Not bad. Where's Ceres?"

From behind a particularly large Alliance officer Ceres stood up. "Here! You're late!"

Brandon was surprised to be the last one of the group in the room, but tried not to wear that on his sleeve. "Well, I…I had a particularly tough time with one of the convicts."

"'One'?" L3-NY laughed. Static crackled from his speaker. "Did I not just brag about my efforts?"

"He had a grudge…" Brandon swung things to another topic. "How are we with the plan?"

"Well," Ceres said. "I managed to make it to the engine room and sabotaged the power supply, the fuel, the propulsion, everything we need, really. Oh! And I disabled the weapons. Which is always handy."

"And as you see, I have gained access to the bridge," L3-NY said. "And I've already plotted our course."

"Fantastico," Brandon smiled. "Time to make our exit."

And with that, he put his fingers in his mouth and whistled, waving the other two to join him as he made his way to the escape pods. Ceres was close behind while L3-NY did a few finishing touches to the ship's controls before leading up the rear.

The trio made their way to the pods and Brandon spun around to instruct his allies. "Okay. Helmets on."

"Yeah, thanks," L3-NY pointed to his mechanical head.

Ceres didn't need to be told twice about putting her helmet on. She knew the plan, and this was the one bit she didn't like the sound of.

Which says something about a plan that involved infiltrating an Eagle-Class Alliance ship where prisoners had escaped and were since rioting.

Brandon nodded as he deployed his own helmet. "Okay!" he turned back to face the escape pod release button. "Let's do this!"

His golden gauntlet smacked against the button and the nearest escape pod jettisoned into outer space, leaving a clear view of the darkness outside the ship.

Until the Second Chance made its way to line up with their exit.

"Are you sure we have to do it like this?" Ceres shouted.

Brandon looked to the princess and smirked. "We don't have the time to double back! It's now or never!"

With that, he leapt out of the Eagle-Class ship and floated towards the starboard door of his own ship.

"This is insane!" Ceres said as she watched the bounty hunter drift towards the opening airlock.

L3-NY took Ceres' hand. "This is Brandon. And he's done worse."

Which was the last thing the droid said before leaping out of the ship and pulling Ceres with him.

Brandon couldn't help but look around as he made his way closer and closer to his ship. Space was so expansive and beautiful it was such a shame he never really spent more time outside of his ship. There was rarely need to – unless he wanted to clean the Second Chance or do repairs – but there were times where he looked out of the window and saw the stars and the very reason he joined the Alliance in the first place. To see the System. To find new worlds.

Now the newest world he found promises a challenge and a worthwhile reward, the need to team up with an old crewmate and a new ally, and the potential of a treasonous group *and* the Alliance wanting his blood.

Which couldn't be better. It had been a long time since life had been this exciting and dangerous. It brought a smile to his face.

The fortune and glory didn't hurt either.

It felt like no time at all when Brandon, L3-NY, and Ceres were all safely back on the ship. Ceres certainly looked a few shades paler than she did back on the Eagle-Class ship, but she was intact.

"Remind me never to do that again," Ceres hiccoughed.

Brandon chuckled and patted her on the back. "Don't worry, princess. It's smooth sailing from now on," the bounty hunter said. "Except, for, you know…the battles we're going to have with those who committed treason against you. And maybe the Alliance. And anyone else who wants to get in our way."

Ceres gazed out the nearby window back at the Alliance ship.
"So, did our plan work?"
"Well, let us see," Brandon folded his arms and joined Ceres in observing.
"Oh, there we go!" L3-NY pointed.
Sure enough, the Eagle-Class ship began to float closer and closer to the other Alliance ships in front of it. Though not travelling that fast, one by one, the smaller ships ahead of the prison transport began to be knocked off-course, the Eagle-Class pinballing between each vehicle.
The path plotted by L3-NY was one that was not intended for any casualties on any part, but one with the desire to sabotage the entire prison convoy of Alliance nearby in order to distract and slow down their work while the Second Chance could be given the opportunity to slip away.
"That wasn't too hard, was it?" Brandon said. He called out to Cherry. "Cherry, activate cloaking and prepare to plot a course."
"Welcome back, Brandon," the ship's A.I. said.
In a snap, the ship finally cloaked without suspicious Alliance eyes on them.
The bounty hunter smiled and took a few steps away from the droid and the princess as he made his way back to the bridge.
"Where to now, Captain?" Ceres asked.
"Well," Brandon paused and wheeled back to the princess. "We're heading to – "
A yellow blur rushed across Ceres and L3-NY's view as it tackled Brandon to the floor. It took a second for everyone to process.
"Falcon!!"
The yellow blur began to punch the bounty hunter over and over again.
It was Ko'Tex.
"Won't you…just give up…already?!" Brandon shouted between punches.
"You imprisoned me!" the Selenian continued to punch.
"What?!" Brandon said. "You're not even on that prison ship any more!"
Ko'Tex paused.
"Oh yeah."
Then the Selenian growled and returned to punching.
"Help!" Brandon called to the duo not doing anything to help. "Someone?"

The bounty hunter was not impressed.

L3-NY raised his gun.

Brandon raised a hand.

"Whoa! No! No shooting!"

Ko'Tex continued. Brandon groaned.

Ceres took a few more steps towards the bounty hunter and the Selenian locked in their brawl and reached into her pocket. The princess pulled out the stun gun Brandon gave her to use on the prison ship and pushed a button to activate it with a constant crackle sound. She didn't need to use it on the Eagle-Class, but she certainly knew how to use it.

Ko'Tex didn't know what hit him. If only he knew the voltage. Almost instantly the Selenian was knocked out. Not being one for personal space, Ko'Tex collapsed onto Brandon, pinning him to the floor even more.

"Ow…" the bounty hunter said.

It took both Ceres and L3-NY to remove the yellow-bodied powerhouse from the crumpled heap of Brandon. But only the bounty hunter was necessary to carry Ko'Tex to the holding cell.

Plus, it gave the chance for Brandon to get a few revenge punches and kicks.

Chapter Twelve

Ko'Tex woke to find himself in the hold of the Second Chance. It wasn't the first time, but hopefully it was the last. In seconds he was already grabbing the bars as he discovered Brandon standing in front of him.

"Rise and shine, my jaundiced friend," Brandon grinned.

"Release me!"

"I already have," the bounty hunter said. "Not that I wanted to, or intended to, but you're free."

"Then why did you put me behind bars?!"

The bounty hunter pointed to the black eye the Selenian gave him. "I don't take kindly to hostility."

Ko'Tex rattled the bars.

"Oh, I wouldn't bother trying that," Brandon said.

"I managed to escape back on that other ship."

"Yeah, well, this is a custom-made holding cell," Brandon said. He raised a remote control. "And I just made a few more modifications."

He pressed the button to release a small electric shock through the metal bars. Ko'Tex recoiled.

"It's just a precaution," the bounty hunter said. "You have a tendency to be…punchy. And stabby and slashy. Not a fan of that…"

Brandon moved over towards a chair that stood nearby and sat on it. "But…I could use that. *We* could use that."

"What are you saying, Falcon?" Ko'Tex nursed his hands and chose not to place them back on the cell's bars.

Brandon leaned forward in his chair. "I want you to join us."

Ko'Tex opened his mouth but Brandon quickly spoke to quieten him. "And before you say it, I'm not part of the Alliance."

Ko'Tex stopped the words Brandon took out of his mouth and chose new ones. "What do you want?"

Brandon rolled the remote in his hand around his fingers. "I would like you to be part of our little team. You see, we have a little mission that could certainly use your help. We need that sort of…mindless, rage-y, loose cannon, psychopathy."

The Selenian's eyes shrunk into slits. He bared his teeth as he spoke to the bounty hunter. "What makes you think I want to help you? Makes you think you can control me? After you *enslaved* me? I am not your *slave*!"

Brandon raised his palms defensively. "Whoa, whoa, there's no slavery going on here! It's just…a business deal."

Ko'Tex's aggression increased yet again. "I don't do business with your kind!" He launched himself against the cell's bars another time. Brandon shook his head and pressed the button in his hand. Another surge of electricity shot through the Selenian in an instant.

"Come on, now, Ko'Tex, don't be a fool…" Brandon paced around the freedom outside the Selenian's cell. The bounty hunter raised the button for Ko'Tex to see. "You're dangerous, *I'm* dangerous, why can't we just be dangerous on the same side for once?…"

The Selenian went to strike the bars, but an inch from doing so, he pulled his strike and held his arm away from the potential surge of pain. Ko'Tex slowly placed his hands around the bars and eased against them in caution. "Falcon, you're even worse than those Alliance dogs."

"Well, thanks?" Brandon shrugged, but then noticed the detail in that last sentence from the Selenian's mouth. "Wait, so now I'm *not* a Alliance dog?"

Ko'Tex grinned in a way that made the bounty hunter rather uneasy. "Alliance dogs wouldn't hide from a fight they know they couldn't win."

The bounty hunter made up the space between himself and Ko'Tex and reached through the bars to grab the Selenian by the throat. He squeezed just enough to prove his position, but not enough to dissuade Ko'Tex from joining his cause.

"You know *nothing* about the way the Alliance are," Brandon said. "Nothing."

Ko'Tex held a shared glare between himself and the bounty hunter. He reached through the bars and pressed the button to engage the electrical modifications Brandon made, and at the drop of a hat volts were surging through the confrontation between the two of them. Both held as firm as they could beyond the uncontrollable twitches and convulsions the surge provided.

It ended as soon as it began, and both sides kept on their feet. Brandon relinquished his grasp on the captive and backed away. "Five hundred thousand credits."

"What do I need your money for?" Ko'Tex sneered. "I deal in honour. And the hunt. And it would be such an honour to hunt you, *Falcon*."

Brandon tossed the button to activate the bar's modifications in the air a couple of times. "Yeah, well, I believe so far I'm winning on our confrontations."

Ko'Tex stepped around his holding cell. "You, you have not beaten me, Falcon…You run from battle! You get your allies to protect you! You hide on the other side of this room because you know I will win!"

The bounty hunter snatched the button from the air and turned his focus entirely on the Selenian. "One day you can have your rematch, Selenian, but for now, if you truly say you deal in honour and the hunt, then why not hunt the least honourable in the System."

Ko'Tex went to open his mouth but Brandon raised a finger to hush him. "That's not me, Ko'Tex, but the bounty my crew are hunting. A planet, Binary, do you know it?"

The Selenian shook his head.

"Neither did I, until a kingdom on its lands contacted me, *persuaded* me to take up a bounty they wanted me to collect," Brandon stood up straight. "Usurpers to the throne. Traitors of their kind."

"And now you want me to help you find them?" Ko'Tex said.

"No, no Ko'Tex, I found them," Brandon nodded. "But I myself were betrayed. It was not usurpers I found in my search, but I found the princess of that kingdom."

Ko'Tex's eyes opened a millimetre. "A princess?"

"'The Lost Princess of Binary Fields'," Brandon said. "Or *Queen*, as she rightfully is."

"And what of her? Where is she now?"

"She…" Brandon paused. "She was the one that incapacitated you with a stun gun."

Ko'Tex instinctively leapt back up in rage.

"But!" Brandon said in the attempt to reign things back in, "But, that means that she needs to regain her rightful place at the throne."

"So you want…to just take her back to this planet?"

Brandon sighed as Ko'Tex was still a while away from catching up. "Well, yes, but there's the small issue of the people who still want to kill her."

"The usurpers of the throne!" Ko'Tex exclaimed. "Where are they?"

Brandon's foot tapped on the floor. "Binary."

"They went back to finish the job?!"

"No, they *are* the job," Brandon shook his head. "The new job. They…Ugh, this is all so complicated and yet not complicated at all."

Ko'Tex was still several steps behind. "And what does this have to do with me?"

Brandon slapped his own forehead and exhaled before he tried another attempt on getting things through to the Selenian. "Okay, look…I took up a bounty to bring in the usurpers to the throne of this Binary place, I find the target, but it turns out it's the lost queen. Then I discover the people who got me to find her were the *real* usurpers to the throne, they just wanted me to find her so they could kill her, but we escaped before they could. After regrouping, the lost queen tasked me with bringing her back, taking down these usurpers, reinstating her in her rightful position, and then I'd be welcome to whatever riches are available to me. But I need help. From the lost queen, a robotic acquaintance and fellow bounty hunter, and hopefully…you."

"What."

"Yeah, it does seem weird when I say it out loud…"

"You need my help to bring down these dishonourable usurpers who deceived you and your code as a bounty hunter?"

"Well…yes," Brandon said. "I could have just said *that*, right?"

"I do not like people without honour," Ko'Tex stated.

"Shock," Brandon said.

"But if you are doing what you say you are doing, then I must help you."

"I could really use that energy you've got," Brandon said. "It's very…violent."

"At one million credits."

Brandon paused. "Wait, you *just* said 'what do I need money for?'!"

"But if you are going to be rewarded untold riches for this task, I demand my own reward too."

"But…honour!"

Ko'Tex shrugged. "It's one million credits."

Brandon didn't have the heart to break it to Ko'Tex that in this situation, one million credits is hardly anything. There was also that part of his bounty hunter brain that kept him from letting onto an even bigger score when he himself could just get a bigger cut. "Deal. Half now, half when the job is done."

The Selenian nodded. "The moment I get that second half, we shall have a rematch. I will wear your skin, Brandon."

"That does not surprise me, and that is gross," the bounty hunter said. He returned to the bars of Ko'Tex's cell and offered his hand to shake.

The Selenian looked at it.

"You...shake it," Brandon said. "It's a human thi–...You know what? Never mind." The bounty hunter removed his hand and made his way out of the room.

"Now that I agreed to help you, Falcon..." Ko'Tex said, tapping his claws on the bars before grasping them. "Release me."

Brandon raised the remote control in his hand and pressed the button one last time. It was the biggest shock to surge through the bars so far, and it was the one that knocked Ko'Tex out once again.

"Maybe after you warm up to me a little more," Brandon said he stepped out into the corridor, the door dropping closed behind him.

Brandon Falcon dropped back into his captain's seat in the bridge and put his feet up. It was a few moments until he realised the attentions of L3-NY and Ceres were on him. The bounty hunter turned to face the neon green bulbs of L3-NY's eye sockets.

"So, did you kill him?" L3-NY asked in a way that would be too perky for a human to say.

"What, no, I didn't!" Brandon brushed off. He laughed for a second until his gaze turned to Ceres.

"Are we going to turn him back in to the Alliance?" Ceres asked, folding her arms.

"Definitely not," Brandon shook his head. "The less we deal with the Alliance, the better. Until it's unavoidable...But we're not returning Ko'Tex to them!"

"Why not? He's a fugitive. They're going to be after us," Ceres said.

"We're not turning him in," Brandon said, before he turned to L3-NY. "And we're not killing him!"

"Awwww..." the droid said.

"I've already done it once, and I'm sure they won't take kindly to me somehow showing up on their doorstep with him again," Brandon explained. "They'll think it's just some long con we're doing."

"Well we've got a con on board!" Ceres said.

"And two bounty hunters, and the lost queen of a planet who wants her dead!"

"Just the usurpers!"

"And how many of them are there!"

"There's–..." Ceres paused. "...a lot."

"There's a lot!" Brandon said. "Wait...How much *is* a lot?"

Ceres showed everything she didn't want to say.

"Oh God," Brandon sat up. "And you want the four of us to take them all down?"

"Wait, 'four'?" L3-NY interjected.

"I've convinced Ko'Tex to help us out."

"You what?!" shouted both Ceres and L3-NY.

Brandon put his feet down and swivelled in his chair to face the two fellow crewmembers in the Second Chance's bridge. "I managed to persuade him to join the cause."

"How?" L3-NY asked.

"You know, honour, the hunt…" Brandon said. "One million credits…"

"One million?!" Ceres said. "Have you not *met* this Selenian before?"

Brandon stood up as he held up his defence. "And just imagine what he'll be like when he meets those people on Binary! Those without honour, full of deception, betrayal, he *hates* people like that!"

"He's probably good in a fight…" L3-NY reasoned to himself.

"He'll be brilliant in a fight!" Brandon said. He pointed at his black eye. "And with the odds against us, we need all the help we can get!"

Ceres shook her head and unfolded her arms. "Can we trust him?"

"Can you trust those people back on Binary?"

"You don't know who they are."

"I know they want you dead, and now you've got three people ready to get in their way!"

L3-NY raised his hand and looked to both the bounty hunter and the princess. "Whoa, wait, yeah, that point right there. That three of us thing, one of them being me…*Three* people? Against…however many people who want to stop us? Also, thank you for calling me a person, Falcon."

"Yeah, well, it was easier to say. But hey, you're still my favourite robot."

"I'm a *droid*, damnit!"

"And here I thought you wanted to be a person. Like in that Robin Williams film."

"Who's Robin Williams?"

"Damnit, does *no-one* on board here do their mandatory homework?!" Brandon said, as far away from the point as he could be in that moment.

Ceres stood up. "You are still oh so wonderful towards helping my cause, Brandon. And I appreciate the effort you've made to recruit both L3-NY and now…this…Selenian…"

"Full disclosure," L3-NY leaned back in his own chair. "It was mostly the money that got the initial hook into me."

"And, yeah," Brandon added, "It was money that interested me in first trying to find you and then to help you."

"Plus, apparently this Selenian guy is getting some credits…"

"But!" Brandon said, trying to put things back on track, "The important thing is that we're here to help you and put things right."

"Even though," L3-NY wanted to remind the rest of the people present, "There are only *three* people ready to help out."

Brandon raised a finger. "Which is exactly why we're going back to Aurora."

"The place," L3-NY said. "That is crawling with the Alliance, who you hate, who I hate, and I'm pretty sure this fugitive we've got in the hold hates too."

"Yes."

"I trust your judgement, Falcon," Ceres said. Even though her face could not offer an attempt to avoid showing otherwise.

"I have a plan," Brandon said. "Which involves going to Aurora. We need more people, and this ship needs one more crewmember."

"And Aurora is the key?" Ceres asked.

"Aurora is our New York City, and we need to complete the assembly of our Avengers."

"So we're called The Avengers now?" L3-NY said in a tone that would be accompanied with a raised eyebrow if he had one.

"Goddamnit, Lenny, we get broadcasts from the Earth of a couple hundred years ago! Do your research on my cultural references!"

"From 200 years ago?"

"We're going to Aurora!" Brandon ended the discussion. He turned his attention on Cherry, the Second Chance's AI. "Cherry! Put us back on course to Aurora!"

"Captain, L3-NY already re-initiated our course to Aurora not long after you boarded the ship," Cherry responded.

Brandon turned to look at L3-NY, who shrugged. "What? I know exactly what you have in mind, Falcon."

"Is that your way of saying you want to be captain?"

"Nope, I've always found this chair to be a lot more comfortable," L3-NY melted into his chair. "Part of the reason I'm not standing like you two are."

The captain looked to the princess and both realised that L3-NY was true in his observation. Ceres soon moved back down into her seat while Brandon was pre-occupied with a thought.

"You're made of metal, you can't feel how comfy that chair is," Brandon said as he sat back down into his captain's seat. The captain made a few adjustments at his controls and looked back out to the far reaches of space that they were travelling through on their way back to Aurora.

"And wait, since when have you been sitting in my chair?"

Chapter Thirteen

It had been quite a journey in the time between Brandon last arriving on Aurora and where he stood flanked by Ceres and L3-NY, looking out the starboard doors, ready to touch down on the surface. The life of a bounty hunter was certainly eventful, but it had been on a completely different level more recently for the captain and his ragtag makeshift crew.

Ko'Tex remained in the hold. Conscious, but still infuriated. At that point, Brandon reasoned that at the state things were in, it would just be more ideal to release him at the best possible moment and point him in a direction they'd like clearing.

It also helped to keep him contained while they were on a planet that was the home base of the very group that held him as a prisoner.

Dust whirled around the Second Chance as it lowered itself slowly and carefully into the hangar they chose to dock in. Brandon held a finger over the door release button; ready to disembark once the slow-moving docking station eventually made its way to align with the Second Chance's magnet strips. They were in a part of the city so full of holes and full of technology years beyond last being put through maintenance that it was a wonder the docking station even had such technology that still worked.

L3-NY spoke up to try and fill the awkward silence as the trio watched the docking station creep towards the starboard door.

"So we have a bounty hunter than never kills, a bounty hunter who sometimes kills, a fugitive who loves to kill, and a princess whom everyone she's ever loved has been killed. What's next, a prisoner prince who kills bounty hunters?"

"Close. An ex-girlfriend," Brandon said.

"Oh, so a four-eyed orange alien who'll only want to kill you. Fantastic."

"It's four arms, but I see your point."

"And you think your ex-girlfriend is going to trust you?" Ceres asked.

"It's Aurora, a planet full of the Alliance and the people the Alliance beat. No-one really trusts anyone. But money? Jobs? Hunting wrong-doers? Those are things people can trust," Brandon explained. He turned to look at the princess. "Why else do you think I ended up becoming a bounty hunter?"

Brandon pressed the button to open the starboard doors and the three of them stepped out into the tunnel that had connected itself to the Second Chance.

It wasn't a port that inspired much confidence. As Brandon looked through the holes in the tunnel's fabric he gazed up at the sun beaming through holes in the hangar's ceiling and walls. It was certainly the best region to lie low on Aurora, but it wasn't exactly the best region for much else.

"I'm sure you've got a lot of reasons why you ended up becoming a bounty hunter," Ceres said as they continued on their way.

"Well, I'd certainly love to hear them, because it was pretty much just the money for me," L3-NY said.

"In case you haven't realised, Ceres," Brandon said, squinting out the harsh sunlight as they left the hangar, "I'm not one for talking about my past. The present, yes. The future, certainly. Any time I'm happy with what I've got and what I'm going to earn, let's talk about that. Right now, however, we've got a job to do."

"Glad to see you're still fun at parties," L3-NY said.

"Hey, I'll have you find that people love me at parties…" Brandon said, a moment before a sniper's bullet struck the ground a metre in front of them. The bounty hunter leapt into action, drawing his Stunderbuss and aiming it high around the surrounding buildings, the princess taking cover behind him.

Meanwhile, L3-NY's sensors where already scanning the trajectory of the sniper bullet in front of them, looking for a read on the origin of the shot. The droid's finger squeezed a hair on his rifle, ready to let off a round in the direction of their aggressor.

"I got 'em, cap," L3-NY said.

"Don't bother, you don't have the range to make that shot."

"Have you forgotten that I'm a droid who can calculate for the shot a countless degree better than any other lifeform?"

"Calculate this."

"You…didn't grab or point to anything."

"We have a woman present," Brandon continued his own manual scan of the surrounding area, before stopping on the tiniest glimpse of orange. "*Two* women."

Brandon took his hand off his Stunderbuss. The bounty hunter lowered his weapon and placed it on the ground before raising his hands. "Do the same," he said to L3-NY.

"What? Why?" the droid wondered. "Did you not hear the part when I said I could–"

Which is all L3-NY said, because he was soon silenced by the second warning shot that zinged a millimetre away from his head.

"I heard everything you said, Lenny," Brandon said. "But so could she." The captain pointed over into the distance. L3-NY turned and focused his sensors in the same direction, and in moments he had the sight of a four-armed orange alien clocked. Brandon leaned towards L3-NY. "And she can see and shoot just as well, too."

The alien – who still had her sights down the scope of her sniper rifle – took this opportunity as an introduction, and waved with her upper right arm for the droid to see.

"*That's* who we're here for?"

"Her name is Tia, and hopefully she's gonna be our final crewmember," Brandon said. He looked up towards the alien who had the two of them trained in her sights. "If she doesn't shoot us first."

"L3-NY! Put your gun down!" Ceres hissed. The princess hadn't gotten as far as she did just to get sniped where she stood by some stranger.

"Yeah, Lenny," Brandon said. "Put your gun down."

"You're enjoying this too much."

"I'm the captain, remember?" Brandon said. He looked around the rest of the surrounding area to make sure there weren't any more snipers hiding about. "My word is law. I do it so I can look after my crew, and look after my…"

Brandon stopped in his tracks when he saw where the second sniper bullet went after it shot past L3-NY's head. "My ship! She shot it! That…she…come on!"

Although he couldn't hear her there and then, he was right in assuming Tia was laughing. A lot.

After time passed and the trio deemed it safe for them to move closer towards the location of the mysterious Tia, Brandon and L3-NY collected their weapons, holstered them, and the three made the trek through the streets of Aurora.

They were in a long vacated area that was ravaged in the Civil War. While Brandon and L3-NY and the rest of the crew of the ill-fated Grasshopper-1135 had joined the Battle for Aurora way above the planet, many battles were had on the planets surface. Guerrilla warfare of a much closer level of brutality and tragedy. It had seemed that Tia had set up home in the region long forgotten by the Alliance, that secret shame of an elephant in the room for whatever Alliance-aligned parents had to deal with an inquisitive child curious of that moment in history.

"…Not that Tia fought in the Civil War. And she never really had a side she agreed with," Brandon explained to Ceres and L3-NY as they progressed through the once war-torn concrete jungle. "I met her long after those days. When I was already a successful bounty hunter."

L3-NY couldn't help but let a laugh escape. "'Successful'…"

"So she's a bounty hunter?" Ceres asked.

"One of the best," Brandon replied.

L3-NY's laugh stopped. "Is she better than me?"

Brandon picked up the laughing. "Well, she's pretty damn good."

"But Brandon, is she better than this?" L3-NY flexed the non-existent muscles all droids lack.

"She's certainly quieter than you," spoke a voice behind the droid. L3-NY froze as he rocked against the touch of a gun barrel.

"Falcon…" L3-NY began. "Please tell me you can throw your voice and I'm leaning up against a pipe…"

"Don't worry, droid," the voice continued. "If I wanted to shoot you I would have done it when you were all lined up in a row."

A hand raised over L3-NY's shoulder and smacked him in the head.

"Ow!"

"Just making the point I'm better than you."

L3-NY's eyes dimmed as he processed his next movements. The droid reached for his gun and manoeuvred his way around in a spin, aiming his weapon towards the stranger's presence. L3-NY's rifle warmed, but not fast enough for two orange hands to grab the barrel of the gun and wrench it away from him while a third hand punched the droid in the chest and the fourth spun a handgun back into its holster so it was free to make an obscene hand gesture.

"Lenny, I'd like you to meet Tia Roma," Brandon said.

L3-NY raised his hands. "I can see why you'd want to date her."

Tia grimaced and tossed the droid's gun back into his hands. Deactivated, of course. She flicked her ponytail of hair trailing behind her as she scratched her shaved head.

"Yeah, well, apparently I was too much to handle," the alien broke her silence.

"It was the hands," Brandon whispered to L3-NY as Tia made her way closer and closer to him.

"What brings you crawling back here?" Tia said.

"I'm not 'crawling back'," Brandon said as Tia – now with four empty hands – approached. "What do you…"

Her lower left and upper right arm grabbed a hold of the captain and her strength made it hard for Brandon to avoid the strong right body blow from her lower left fist and the sting of the slap from her upper left hand.

This was all followed by a swift knee that brought Brandon down to his knees. Tia stepped back as the winded bounty hunter crawled a little as he tried to recover.

Ceres moved past the grounded Brandon and stood eye to eye with Tia. "Hey!" she shouted. "I don't know who you are, but…"

Tia eyed her up and down and chuckled. "So you're Falcon's latest prey? Cute."

"What? No…I'm…"

"Cute," Tia winked.

"Please don't tell me she's like Falcon but with twice as many arms," L3-NY said.

"Hey! I am not like Falcon! If anything, he's like me!" Tia defended. She reached down and picked Brandon up by the shoulders, standing him back up on his feet. "Without me he wouldn't have half the stuff he has as a bounty hunter! None of the skill, none of the fancy toys, not even that ship!"

"Okay, now you're crazy, that's always been his ship," L3-NY said.

"And who do you think was the mechanic skilled enough to get that bucket of bolts back in the sky again?" Tia argued. She looked to Ceres and L3-NY. "You don't seriously think Falcon got where he did without help, do you?"

Tia gave Brandon another punch to wind him. "Typical ungrateful Alliance drop-out. You help them, you train them, you fall for them, you fix their ship and boom, 'All of space is out there Tia, I'm sorry, it's calling me!'"

"Tia," Brandon struggled back onto his feet. "I need your help."

"Oh really? Help you out so you can just leave again and fly around on your little space adventures!" Tia paced side to side. "I don't need to help you, I'm a bounty hunter too! What could you possibly say to try and convince me?"

"A bounty. A big one. The biggest."

"Yeah, yeah, I'm not going to help you find some alien…"

"The bounty is a planet."

"Huh?"

Brandon dusted himself off.

"Binary. A planet with a stolen throne at the head of its kingdom, and the promise of countless riches for the task of establishing its rightful heir," he explained.

Tia weighed up the information. Her eyes looked to Brandon and his two companions. "And you think the three of you…"

"Four of us," Brandon corrected. "We have a Selenian."

"A Selenian?" Tia couldn't believe it. "How did you get one of them?"

"We made him angry, and then we stunned him," Brandon said. "And made him more angry…But then more stunning!"

"*Four* of you are on a hunt to solve the problem of a planet that isn't your own. For what, money?"

"Lots and lots of money!" L3-NY nodded. Brandon sighed.

"Just…feels like the right thing to do," Brandon said.

Tia's eyes narrowed as she looked at the way Brandon was acting. She raised a finger. "Wait. It's not just the money, and it's not about doing the right thing…"

She stepped closer, almost colliding with the stationary Brandon. Her eyes zoned in on the captain.

"Huh," Tia acknowledged. "That's the fire of the Brandon I knew."

Ceres and L3-NY looked to each other to try and determine an answer to what Tia meant, but both just shrugged. Then Tia swung a fist towards Brandon that drew their attention.

But Brandon snatched the fist out of the air. "So is that a yes to helping us?"

The captain pushed Tia's fist away and took a step back. The edge of the alien's lip rose. "Try to land a punch on me. If you can do that before I can land one on you, I'll humour your little call to adventure."

"Oh come on, Tia, I have no time for this," Brandon rolled his eyes. "We've got a job to do – " the bounty hunter said, absent-mindedly drawing his Stunderbuss. He fired from the hip, distracting Tia from the point through his speech, but…nothing happened.

Brandon looked down to his gun. He pulled the trigger again. And again. Click. Click. Nothing. He looked to Tia.

"Well, this is awkward."

Tia laughed and revealed the power supply of the Stunderbuss in one of her hands.

"You're too predictable, Falcon," Tia said. "And you didn't think to consider just how easy it is for me to disarm you."

"Well, you do have more…arm…" Brandon tried to retort.

The alien sneered and tossed the power supply to Ceres, who managed to catch it on short notice. Brandon exhaled and pushed the Stunderbuss into L3-NY's hands and rushed towards Tia.

The captain swung his first punch; an obvious open Tia saw a mile away. The four-armed female snatched the fist out of the air and monkey-tossed Brandon across the dust. Brandon rolled into the throw and with a bounce-up to his feet, perfectly timed to grab an approaching Tia.

In a grapple, Tia and Brandon swung side-to-side, either one trying to get the other off balance. A foot rose off the ground here and there, but for the most part, it was an even grapple.

Of course, when you have two pairs of arms, you still have the unfair advantage. Which is what Tia took advantage of. Using her lower arms to grab and pin Brandon's arms to his sides, the alien allowed herself to use her upper fists to throw punches.

But Brandon was ready for this. Tia's attacks were too heavy and orchestrated, not as refined as they could be. It was the desperation to get the first blow rather than exercise finesse. Something Brandon could exploit through reading the telegraphed blows, swinging his head and whatever freedom his body still had to avoid being punched in the face.

Pulling his legs together and his knees up, Brandon managed to maneuver a way to kick away from Tia, all the while wriggling and otherwise attempting to slip out of the clutches of his aggressor. Breaking the hold, Brandon's back slammed against the rough floor while a stumbling Tia bumped against L3-NY, dropping the Stunderbuss to the ground.

Brandon groaned as he pulled himself back up to face his opponent, who was already swift on the way to attack yet again. The bounty hunter dodged and dived punches here and there. His body pivoted and swung in avoidance of arcs Tia's fists travelled in. He tried to regain an upper aggressive ground, meeting each punch he avoided with one of his own to keep Tia at bay, but it was only a temporary fix.

In realization of a futile task, Brandon looked past Tia in the milliseconds that he had free, and registered his Stunderbuss' position on the ground. The bounty hunter leapt past the alien, and was a metre away from being reunited with his weapon before his foot was snatched out of orbit by one of Tia's hands.

On the brink of being reeled back in and probably punched a lot more than once, Brandon spun around as fast as he could. He looked up and saw the smile increasing on Tia's face as she saw victory soon coming, but Brandon continued the fight.

He kicked Tia's hand and used his arms to pull himself along the ground, away from her and closer to his trusty gun. Patting around behind him – his eyes not taking a second to look away from Tia – Brandon soon felt the welcome cool of the metallic weapon.

"Ceres! Throw me that!" Brandon called to the Princess, an open palm calling for the power supply of the Stunderbuss. Without wondering on the request, Ceres tossed the item back towards the captain.

Though Tia's arms got their first.

With an interception, Tia managed to stop Brandon's attempt on using his tools to an advantage.

"Oh, Brandon," Tia teased. "I just can't tear you away from that Stunderbuss for a second, can I?"

With a clench of her fist, the power supply of the Stunderbuss crunched and broke into pieces. No power supply, no ability to take Tia down in a flash.

"What other gadgets are you going to have to pull out of your backside to take me down, I wond–" Tia began, but was interrupted by the L3-NY running towards her, clocking her jaw with a fist of his own and bringing her to the floor.

"Boom! Victory!" L3-NY said, gesturing his accomplishment.

Tia sat on the lowered cargo door of the Second Chance. A towel that contained ice was placed against her jaw that had resisted against the metallic blow that was L3-NY's robotic fist.

"Well," Brandon said, rubbing his prickly chin, "You didn't explicitly say who had to land a punch on you."

"I think that if I were not the person I am, I would have a problem with your bending of the rules, Falcon."

Brandon shrugged. "Hey, I had it all under control. L3-NY was the one who did the punching."

"And what a punch he has," Tia said. She spat some blood to the ground and adjusted the ice she placed against her face.

"So, what do you say?" Brandon asked. "We took on your challenge. We won…technically…"

Tia looked to him for a second, and then shook her head.

"You need a lot more than just me," Tia said. "However awesome I might be."

"Well can you help us with getting more people?"

Tia appreciated that little joke to her ears. "You remember what planet you're standing on, right?" Tia passed the ice back to Brandon and she stood up. "Getting me was hard. Getting all the scum on Aurora looking for a quick buck will be like shooting a para-rat with your eyes shut."

L3-NY spoke up. "So, difficult?"

Tia drew her pistol in a slick motion, swung it behind her and let off a single shot. A para-rat flapping past the ship fell towards the dirt. Dead.

"That didn't answer anything," L3-NY said. "That looked difficult. Was that difficult?"

The journey across Aurora through the back-roads and the districts long forgotten since the War felt lengthy, but it went without a hitch. L3-NY and Ceres hitched a ride on Tia's speeder as she led the way, Brandon not far behind on his hoverboard.

It wasn't long until Tia pulled up outside the Gilded Diamond, with Brandon leading up the rear, surprised by how quick their journey was.

"Wow, I'm surprised by how quick that was," Brandon commented.

"Not the first time you've said that," Tia muttered.

"'The Gilded Diamond?'" Ceres read the sign above her. "Why cover a diamond in gold? That's kinda counter-productive…"

"I know, right?" Brandon said, as they made their way through the entrance. "That's exactly what I said…"

In the moment they stepped inside the best worst bar around, things ground to a halt. Everyone went silent at the line-up of a bounty hunter, a droid, an alien with four arms, and the most unlikely female to be found in a place like the Gilded Diamond.

"Um…Hi," Brandon waved.

In the following moment, countless guns and other weapons un-holstered and found their way to being armed and aimed towards the bounty hunter and his crew.

"Wow, Brandon, what did you do?" Tia asked, raising all four palms.

"Why are you surrendering?" L3-NY said, his hands firm on his gun.

"How did we get into this mess?" Ceres wondered.

"The real question is who are they actually after?" Brandon looked around the room. "And when are they going to shoot?"

"Does anyone have a plan?" Tia asked.

"Yes," Brandon nodded. Then he raised his palms as he addressed the Gilded Diamond. "Don't. Shoot."

Silence.

And then laughter erupted through the bar. One by one, weapons disengaged and little by little, noise and activity filled the Gilded Diamond.

"What is going on?!" Ceres asked, confused by the entire occasion.

The four of them relaxed and Brandon made his way towards the bar. To be more accurate, he moved towards a notice board behind the bar for all to see. The bounty board.

At a glance, all questions were answered. Brandon couldn't help but smile when the realisation dawned on him.

"I've made it," he said. The bounty hunter turned to face the others. "I'm on the bounty board!"

His companions followed his lead and moved closer to see what Brandon was talking about. Sure enough, there was a mug shot of Brandon being used for a bounty poster. The captain stood proudly and made an impression of his face on the sheet of paper. Brandon was a little more rugged and unkempt than the photo, but then again, it had been quite a journey recently, especially with said photo coming from his old Alliance record.

L3-NY began to laugh. Brandon's face fell. "Hey, what's so funny?"

L3-NY didn't say anything until he started to point at the bottom of the poster and hunch over. Droids couldn't run out of breath, but L3-NY continued with the motions to add more weight to them.

"Look at how much you're going for!"

Brandon spun back towards the poster and his eyes bulged. Angry, he moved closer and pointed at the amount offered for his bounty.

"24,000 Credits?!" Brandon yelled. "I'm worth more than that!!"

Tia joined L3-NY in the laughter and patted Brandon on the back. "Really? What have you been doing that's so great, Falcon?"

"This isn't fair, I'm a damn good bounty hunter! One of the best!"

L3-NY and Tia continued in their hysterics. Brandon had enough, and retired to getting a drink. Ceres looked to the three of them.

"Um, everyone?..." Ceres said. "What about the mission?"

L3-NY and Tia chuckled and made their way to sit next to Brandon. Tia ordered a large tankard while L3-NY ordered nothing, because he was a droid.

Ceres folded her arms, unimpressed. If she hadn't been so far away from the Second Chance and hadn't had to rely on the others to bring her around the System, she would have left. Instead, she made her way over to the small stage on the other side of the building, where several drunken customers practised the universal past time of karaoke in traditional ineptitude.

She did not head to that area to sing, however. Instead, she took the microphone when a male Taran stumbled off to buy another five drinks for himself.

With a rush of feedback and a high-pitched whine from the speakers grabbing everyone's attention out of the aural pain, Ceres cleared her throat and spoke into the microphone.

"Um. Hi," Ceres said. One by one, patrons of the Gilded Diamond turned their attentions back to whatever originally had their attentions. It didn't deter Ceres from continuing. "You don't know me, but I have a job for whoever needs one."

"Yeah? What for, shining your shoes?" someone heckled.

The bartender brought Brandon and Tia their drinks. Interested by Ceres' action, the bounty hunter picked up his drink and downed it rather quickly, an eye resting on Ceres continued address.

"You see," Ceres said. "I, I...*We* need people. Good people."

"Good luck finding them here!"

"Pilots. People who can fight. My home planet, Binary..."

"I've never heard of it!"

"...Is in trouble. And I am the lost queen, entitled to my rightful place..."

"She's had more than I have!"

"…I know it sounds crazy, but they killed my family and tried to kill me…"

"Why did she come to Aurora of all places?"

"…I had to run away, but I can only imagine what the innocent people trapped on the planet have to live with…"

"Why doesn't she just go to Alliance, they seem to look after rich, entitled cry babies…"

"…So I found some people willing to help, but it still won't be enough. There's only five of us. We can't just go down there…"

"What, Falcon and that lot?…"

Brandon finished his drink and pulled himself back up, dragging his bar stool out of the way. He started to walk through the jeering customers, towards Ceres.

"…Which is why I thought maybe we could use your help. Whoever wants to help. Those who do I can reward…"

"Yeah? How much?"

Brandon hopped onto the stage and leant into the microphone. "One million credits."

He paused for effect.

"Each," he finished.

Silence.

And then everyone leapt to life. Ceres put her hand over the microphone and mouthed: "'Each?'…"

Brandon waved away her concerns. "Bounty hunters only speak in money. And thankfully, I'm fluent in it."

"But…*Each*?"

"Why, do you not have that many credits?" Brandon asked.

"That's just a lot of credits, that's all. Depending on whether anyone wants to actually help us."

L3-NY and Tia walked up to the two of them. The alien sipped at her tankard while the aperture over L3-NY's eyes opened and his eyebulbs brightened with concern. "One million credits each? I better be getting a raise!"

"Raise?" Tia's eyebrow lifted. "This droid has been paid already?"

"I have a name."

"You have a model number," Tia said, before squinting to see the markings on L3-NY's back.

"Yeah! That's…also my name…"

"Lenny, don't listen to her," Brandon told L3-NY. "Tia, Lenny needed to be swayed by being paid in advance. Just like you had to put me through some fight of honour or something."

"You got this droid to finish the fight for you!"

"I didn't ask him to. And besides, honour among thieves. Even though we don't steal things."

"You stole my leg once!" L3-NY reminded Brandon.

"Point is, Lenny needed money, you needed closure on how much of a badass I am, Ko'Tex…needed several thousand volts put through his body…And now look at us. Here, right now, about to have try-outs to see who else wants to join."

"…Try-outs?"

Calling the process of recruiting bounty hunters and whatever other money-hungry clientele of the Gilded Diamond "try-outs" was a fair bit of poetic licence. In reality, it boiled to an exchange that almost always went:

"Have you come to volunteer your services for The Binary Bounty?"

"Are you really offering one million credits each?"

Eyes may or may not roll at that point. Then:

"Yes."

"I'm in."

"Good," followed by digits scrawled down on a bar napkin. "Meet us at these co-ordinates and await further instructions. This is going to be a life-changing bounty for everyone, so try and stay in one piece until then."

A good percentage of the bar patrons signed up in a short amount of time. There wasn't much more one needed to do to convince the desperate side of Aurora to act on such a crazy goal. Money talked. Adventure helped, but it was really those digits that swayed most.

Most.

A trio of bounty hunters made their way up to Brandon and company's makeshift recruitment desk.

"Falcon, Falcon, Falcon," the Trogian bounty hunter in front of him spoke. "How is it you've gone from your usual bounties to the big leagues? What is it you're not telling us?"

He flexed his arms, the pelts of victims past swaying in the air conditioning.

L3-NY sighed at the display, static rushing out of his speaker. The droid stood up and excused himself.

"I'm gonna get a drink."

"Ah, gentlemen," Brandon deadpanned to the hunters that joined them. "Good to see you again. Is this a sign that you'd like to put yourself up for collecting on this bounty?"

"If your little girlfriend out here isn't just talking crazy, she's definitely still talking about insanity," the Halorian bounty hunter mused. "Saving a kingdom? A *planet*?"

A platinum sword swung its way down into the table the crew of the Second Chance sat at. The Selenian who owned it yanked the blade back out and brandished it.

"And Falcon over here wants us to do his dirty work," the Selenian mocked. "The bounty hunter who never kills."

Tia yawned and drew her pistol. Switching it from hand to hand, she eventually had it pointed right between the Selenian's eyes. "He already has a crew of questionable morals. And one too many Selenians to deal with already. So keep it quiet."

The Selenian chuckled. "I see this one has attitude," he said, before turning his sights over to the princess. "And this is the lost queen of this Binary place, right? You seem a little too pretty to be in a place like this…"

He reached out to touch her face, but Ceres pushed a button and the vibro-short sword she had on her flashed to life. The blade flicked mere inches away from the Selenian's hand, which just managed to halt its path.

"It's been a whirlwind of a journey, friend," Ceres said. "And I just want to go home."

"Cute," the Selenian said. The blade-like claw all Selenians possessed flicked out of the back of his hand, millimetres from Ceres' eye. Before the others could react, the Selenian pulled back his arm to strike.

"Hey Toth'To," said the voice of the hand that caught the Selenian's arm before it took a swipe at Ceres.

The Selenian turned his head and saw L3-NY standing next to him.

"I'm a droid," L3-NY's neon eyes narrowed. "I don't drink."

And then he swung a punch that hit Toth'To square in the face, knocking him backwards into his chair and then down to the floor.

"What is it with you and punching all of a sudden?!" Brandon yelled.

L3-NY moved back towards his vacant seat like it was nothing.

"Oh, Toth'To and I have unfinished business," L3-NY explained. "But since maybe he could help us out, I chose not to kill him."

Brandon's eyes opened. "Kill him?!"

"Relax, I *wasn't* gonna kill him," L3-NY waved away. "Scare him, probably. But – "

Is the last sentence L3-NY uttered, because with a swing of his platinum sword, the Halorian bounty hunter sliced the droid's head clean off the rest of his body.

"Lenny!" Brandon called, leaping to his feet, Stunderbuss drawn. The Trogian stepped into his path.

"I'm okay!" called a voice from under the table. "I'm okay! I'm just…a little bit shorter right now…"

Tia looked under her feet and found L3-NY's head, still functional. She picked him up and looked towards the captain and the Trogian staring each other down, then to the smug-looking Halorian.

"Turn me around!" L3-NY said up to Tia. "My head! Spin me around and let me see the coward who did that!"

At his request, Tia rolled L3-NY around in her hands and held him up to look at the Halorian. His green LEDs flashed and changed. "Oh, you are so in trouble once I get back to my body. I'll knock you out too."

The Halorian sneered. "Well it's a shame there's nothing you can do about your bucket of bolts right now."

"I…" L3-NY conceded to the Halorian bounty hunter's point. "You're right. There's nothing I can do about my body right this second.

"But she can."

Ceres looked to L3-NY's standing robotic body and then looked towards the Halorian. Acting as a puppet master through her technopathy, she manipulated and controlled the servos and other machinery that made L3-NY such an articulate and skilled physical powerhouse of a bounty hunter droid.

The Halorian never even realised L3-NY's body seemingly coming to life without his head attached. The droid's torso spun on its pelvis to face the cowardly attacker, followed by L3-NY snatching the Halorian's wrist and simultaneously twisting and squeezing it. A few snaps and breakages in seconds later, Ceres made L3-NY's other hand grab the falling platinum sword out of the air, leading to L3-NY's body to spin almost a full 360 degrees with weapon in hand, narrowly stopping at the blade nicking the antagonist's neck.

"Whoops," Ceres said.

The Halorian put his hands up. One of them flopped, wrist completely broken. It did not deter the towering Trogian, who stood up even straighter to flourish his true size and intimidating stance. But Brandon did not back down. He did, however, lower his Stunderbuss.

The Trogian laughed. "You sure have the selection of friends, *Brandon*."

"And I think we're becoming fast ones, too."

"Seems like you and your four-armed freak haven't done anything though. And to think, you two looked to be the only useful ones in your group."

Brandon shrugged, putting his hands in his pocket. "Yeah, well, I guess I can take your lame attempt to insult us, but you're also saying you don't agree with the great Tia Roma. Bounty hunter legend."

A spit to the ground confirmed the Trogian's ignorance. "Yeah, like the great Tia Roma was a woman."

L3-NY's head was carefully placed on the table with a tap as Tia got out of her seat.

"Well, she still is, scrub," Tia said as she stood behind the Trogian. "And I've been collecting bounties larger than your life savings from when you were just a cry baby on a sand dune."

The Trogian shook his head as he turned around to face Tia. "Tough words coming from a freak."

"It's called the System, bog-breath," Tia wafted away the smell from her nostrils and cracked all of her knuckles. "Intergalactic diversity. But it seems idiocy is universal."

"What are you going to do? Punc– "

Tia didn't so much punch the Trogian as she did deliver a machine gun volley of blows to all of the hunter's pressure points. It was a handy skill to have as a bounty hunter and even more so in a bar brawl. But Tia couldn't have all of the fun.

Using her hands to stabilise the groggy Trogian, Tia spun the hunter around to face Brandon once more. Off-balance, stepping side-to-side and forward and back, the hunter wobbled on his feet while Brandon planned his three-step attack.

Step One: Punch the Trogian clean in the gut, causing him to hunch over.

Step Two: Engage the bulletproof bubble that deployed around Brandon's head from his suit, offering an improvised headbutt assist.

Step Three: Headbutt.

If there were a Step Four, it would be stand back and bask in the small victories life offers. Like headbutting Trogian's in their big heads and making them collapse onto their butts.

With the trio of rude bounty hunters dazed and confused around the floor of the Gilded Diamond, Brandon and the others determined that it would be the perfect time for them to leave.

"I think that's the perfect time for us to leave," Brandon said. Placing down some Credits to pay for the disturbance. Tia nodded and gestured for Ceres to follow. The princess agreed, picking up L3-NY's head on the way out.

The captain clapped his hands together and addressed the rest of the bar as they stepped over the Trogian, Selenian, and Halorian. "Those of you who are answering our call…and the one million credit each bounty…you know where to go! We shall see you then, but for now, we are going to be on our way. Drink up. Adventure will follow – "

And – Brandon discovered as he stepped out of the Gilded Diamond's doors – as did the Alliance.

A squad of Alliance soldiers held their formation outside the doors of the bar. It was a surprising sight to behold, since the Alliance barely ever found their way to that area of Aurora, not the least in the number that had assembled in front of the crew of the Second Chance.

"Well," Brandon observed, "This can't be good."

The senior officer took a step towards the group.

"I believe you are exactly who we're looking for," the officer said. Brandon backed away.

"Hey, not cool, man," Brandon said. "The Alliance aren't in the bounty hunting business, if you've come to collect me, it's definitely not fair."

The Alliance officer shook her head.

"Oh no, I did not realise you had a bounty on your head…whoever you are…" her eyes scanned Brandon up and down in judgement. "But your appearance has raised flags in our systems."

"Come again?"

The Alliance officer smiled. "This is Aurora. Did you not realise that we have surveillance all across this planet, not to mention a good chunk of the System?"

"The System's changed since I once knew it," Brandon's fists clenched.

With a nod, the Alliance officer continued. "Well, our facial recognition software has determined that you have impersonated an Alliance officer and are harbouring a dangerous fugitive."

Brandon didn't break as he looked over the surrounding squad. They were armed, but all weapons were holstered.

Tia moved to Brandon's side and muttered into his ear. "Alliance response times aren't ever that fast."

Brandon judged the group facing them. Something was off. "What's your badge number?"

"DEC-7241-A," replied the Alliance officer.

Brandon paused. Then shook his head.

"Okay, that meant nothing to me."

The officer smiled. It was one of those smiles reserved for customer service servicing incorrect customers.

"Please come with us to Alliance Hall peacefully, and we can all deal with this matter civilly."

Brandon nodded as though he was agreeing to the peaceful terms, but something still wasn't quite right.

"Alliance don't usually make domestic calls like this, and surely, if you think we're harbouring a dangerous fugitive, you'll see they aren't here," Brandon said. His fingers tapped at his gauntlets. "We're just a ship's crew, having a drink as we make port in Aurora. We come in peace."

The officer tilted her head to one side. "If you come in peace, then why are you armed?"

"I could say the same question."

"We're the Alliance. We need to keep the peace, especially on our base planet."

Brandon shook his head as his hand went towards his Stunderbuss. "No. *They're* the Alliance," Brandon nodded past the officer and her squad towards a separate group of Alliance officers running towards them. "And it looks like *you're* the one impersonating an Alliance officer. So tell me…" he said, raising his Stunderbuss. "Who are you, and why do you know so much about where we came from?"

Everyone's attentions turned as the doors of the Gilded Diamond flung open. The Halorian, Selenian, and Trogian stumbled their way outside, weapons in their hands. The Trogian bounty hunter felt his forehead and rubbed around it.

It began to flicker. Malfunction. The alien head began to resemble that of a human. Binarian. It was Virgil.

"Falcon!"

"You!" Brandon pointed at the Trogian that rapidly began looking less and less Trogian. "I forgot your name, but...*you*!"

Virgil pointed to command the two bounty hunters that flanked him. As well as the imposter Alliance members the other side of Brandon and the others. "Get them! Kill the princess!"

"Time to go!"

Brandon put his fingers into his mouth and whistled while his other hand reached to his side, pulling out a repulsor orb. With a flick of the wrist, Brandon launched the orb towards Virgil and his escorts, knocking them either side of the entrance of the Gilded Diamond. It wasn't before long when gunfire erupted all around the bar's exterior. Both the Alliance and the imposters exchanged shots while a momentarily disabled Virgil and partners got back onto their feet. By the time they had, Brandon and the others had already sprinted back into the Gilded Diamond.

"Why are we going back *inside*?" L3-NY's head asked as he bounced in Ceres' hands.

"Everyone! Scatter!" Brandon called to the bar patrons as he ran past, waving his arms.

As Tia and Ceres followed, L3-NY called out. "No! Stop! My body! Pick up my body!"

The alien hopped to a stop and spun to look at the motionless body to L3-NY's disembodied head. She groaned and rushed over to it, picking it up and draping it behind her back with her lower arms holding it up.

When Tia turned back and rushed after Brandon and Ceres and L3-NY's head, the door to the Gilded Diamond blasted open, with Virgil not far behind, weapon in hand. The rest of the bar sprung to life, yet again drawing their weapons and engaging in the already raging firefight.

"What is happening?!" L3-NY called as Ceres followed Brandon as he pushed open the back door to once again escape to the outside.

Brandon tossed a cube into the air and jumped, timing it so he landed smoothly onto the deployed hoverboard. The bounty hunter swept the board around to face his crew right behind him.

"Tia, take your speeder and bring the others back to the Second Chance. I'll hold them off as much as I can."

"The Second Chance is miles away!" Ceres said.

Brandon smirked and shook his head. "No it's not."

The bounty hunter pointed to the sky where they saw the Second Chance in the distance, making its way to their position, with Cherry using her A.I. to pilot the ship through Aurora's airspace.

And then they saw as shots began to be fired on Brandon's ship.

"Well that's never good," Brandon lowered his finger. "We better hurry."

Brandon drew his Stunderbuss as Tia, Ceres, and the two parts of L3-NY moved over to the speeder. With the rest of his crew in transit, Brandon pointed the hoverboard back to all of the commotion, and begun.

The bounty hunter hovered around the outside of the Gilded Diamond, and using only his Stunderbuss, he began to engage the Alliance and the imposter Alliance soldiers, not picking a side. With the manoeuvrability of the board, he was allowed the freedom to dodge and pivot and dart between the formations, catching people off guard with shots to their sides or their backs, each shot from the Stunderbuss rendering them incapable of fighting.

He had no idea what was going on, but Brandon knew that with the fight worsening and the Alliance being involved, things weren't going to be easy. Brandon aimed towards the very middle of the battle, swinging his Stunderbuss to sweep and trip some of the aggressors up as he sped on by, and he took pot shots on assorted goons just to help lower numbers.

The sound of the approaching Second Chance filled Brandon with the feeling of warmth and comfortable escape, but the noise of increasing intensity of fire onto his prized ship put the apprehension in his chest. He moved around to look at his prized ship as it crawled through the sky about and smiled. With a spin of his gun, Brandon was ready to let off a few more incapacitating shots, but his attention jolted to the body that was thrown out of the nearby window towards him.

It was Virgil, relatively unscathed by the look of things. To Brandon's reckoning, the Binarian must have done well to survive the way he did in the Gilded Diamond, but the sign of the other Binarians rushing out of the bar, as well as a few other stragglers, things were made rather clear what happened.

And as the Gilded Diamond – the best worst bar in Aurora – exploded with a force strong enough to knock everyone in the area off their feet, Brandon knew he was way over his head.

The captain of the Second Chance rolled side-to-side as the cool rush of blood from the back of his head poured drop by drop from the blow he received when the explosion threw him to the floor.

By his feet, Brandon's eyes painfully rolled down to see the damaged hoverboard, sparks and lights flashing to indicate it was beyond simple repair. The bounty hunter groaned as he rolled onto his back, as saw as all varieties of ship rose from ground level and shot into the sky. Whoever managed to escape from the bar made a wise decision to get away from the escalating trouble as soon as possible.

Above Brandon, he saw the Second Chance swaying and attempting to avoid the increasing firepower concentrated on it. Brandon tried to raise a hand towards the ship, but he was still too taken aback from the blast. The captain could barely utter a sound as he helplessly watched as the Second Chance had to make a break away from there, lest the shots it was taking prove to be too much.

He turned to his right where his trusty Stunderbuss sat a metre away. Brandon breathed and reached towards it, his fingers pulling against the rough ground to move himself closer.

But someone else got to it first. Virgil. The Binarian smirked as he kicked the Stunderbuss away from Brandon, before he picked it up for the bounty hunter to watch.

"Oh Mr Falcon," Virgil said. "We put so much faith in you. But I guess that was our first real mistake."

The Binarian took the Stunderbuss and pointed it to Brandon's chest.

"But our mistakes end now."

And things turned to black from Brandon as he got a full taste of his own medicine.

Chapter Fourteen

Brandon came to on a ship that was definitely not the Second Chance. Everything around him was smooth and streamlined. If he didn't travel the System where anything was possible, he would have determined that it was a ship from the future. But as it stood, Brandon found himself in a ship that was not his own, full of white and electric blue, a potentially hostile crew aboard, and his hands locked together in restraints.

"Oh. Oh that's *really* not good," the bounty hunter said, pulling his arms away to try and free himself from the cuffs. They weren't Alloy Cuffs like the ones he used when hunting for bounties, but they seemed to do a good enough job.

Brandon looked around for a way out of his current situation. There weren't many options with his arms restrained and the looks of the cell he was in, but he still kept a keen eye about. It was then when Virgil made his way around the corner.

"You!" Brandon shouted. "Where are we?! I mean, we're on your ship, I know that…But where's my ship? I want to be back on my ship!"

Virgil smirked as he took a seat across from Brandon.

"To our knowledge, your bucket of bolts is fine," Virgil noted. "But we wouldn't dare reunite you with her. But you leave us at a loss, bounty hunter…You didn't hold up your end of the deal."

"Well, I didn't sign up for the job you sold to me, and I'm pretty sure you've been trying to kill me, so…"

Virgil bared his teeth in his grin, a look that wasn't entirely pleasing to the bounty hunter.

"All you had to do was taking care of the princess," Virgil said. "We could have allowed for you just to bring her back to us since you have that silly rule against killing…But saving her and running away was certainly the exact opposite of what we'd have liked."

As Brandon and Virgil spoke, the captain continued to try and slip is way out of his restraints. But they didn't budge. He looked around the ship for any makeshift weapons he could use against the Binarian as some way to forge an escape, but the interior design didn't offer many options.

Annoyed, the bounty hunter started to out the window to try and ascertain a location via the stars or any landmarks in the System, but it was for the most part futile.

Then he saw something. Metallic. Dark. Green lights. A hand. Waving.

L3-NY.

Outside of the ship. Clinging to it by the looks of things.

Brandon had to stop himself muttering "What the…" as the Binarian continued to talk.

"But I digress. I'm sure I don't need to outline our entire plan."

"Oh please do," Brandon chimed in, before looking back to L3-NY.

"I don't think that'll be the case," Virgil said.

"Well I can assume what the next step of your plan will be," Brandon said.

Virgil raised a curious eyebrow.

"Is that so? Enlighten me."

"Well…" Brandon said, eyes flicking over to the sight of L3-NY the other side of the window across the ship. The droid had resorted to some rather bad charades to try and communicate what the captain should do. They involved the droid's fingers counting down, a lot of pointing, a gesture that looked like fireworks, and curling into a ball.

Brandon tried not to give the game away as he tried to decipher L3-NY's wordless message. The bounty hunter felt like he had gotten the gist. But the sight of L3-NY floating away from the ship wasn't what he expected was going to happen.

"…Capturing me…" Brandon said as he got back to recounting his thought of the Binarians' plan. "…Was of course bait. I mean, I'm sure you're not complex and complicated enough to think of something much more than using me to get to the Second Chance and Ceres."

Virgil laughed and nodded. "True, it just seemed simple to rely on your crew to come back and save the captain they know is still alive. For now."

"Right," Brandon said with a look to the window. There was nothing. L3-NY had disappeared. "Why bother doing anything more than just that?"

"Though I have to say, with the crew you've assembled…it's a wonder if they actually would try and rescue you."

"I did the best with what I could, and I think I did pretty darn well."

"So you didn't think they were going to just fly away in your ship?"

Brandon shook his head. Though he did consider the possibility of L3-NY stealing the Second Chance. Or at least his leg back. "Honour among thieves."

Virgil's fingers tapped against his knee.

"Well then, I guess they will be here any minute."

Brandon grinned. "Maybe they're already here. The Second Chance has some pretty darn good cloaking to it. It's amazing that it's gotten this close without you noticing."

Virgil stood up. "So it would be a shame that we saw it coming a mile away."

Brandon's smugness froze. Virgil lowered his head and turned it snake-like towards the bounty hunter. "We've been on your ship before, Falcon. Did you really think we didn't put a trace on you? Why do you think we found you when you returned to Aurora?"

"Why not come for us sooner?" Brandon asked.

"Well it's curious how all those other scrapes you've been in hadn't already done the job for us. You're a lucky man, Brandon Falcon, but I guess we had to finish the job we started all that time ago."

Brandon sat up a little as L3-NY came back into view. The droid was approaching the window rather swiftly, with something boosting him in their general direction.

"Don't count my luck out just yet," Brandon said, hitting his chest with his restrained hands, deploying the protective bubble around his head. Virgil finally turned his head in the direction the bounty hunter was looking, and saw the droid getting close. The bounty hunter reached towards the momentarily distracted Binarian with his bound hands, ready to grab him in a chokehold, but the moment he sprung was the moment his cuffs raised to the ceiling and locked in place.

Virgil turned around.

"Oh Falcon," he said. "Did you seriously think that distraction was going to be enough?"

"Well…clearly I don't now," the bounty hunter said, his arms struggling and wriggling as his wrists remain pressed towards the magnetic ceiling.

Brandon braced for whatever it was L3-NY had planned next. It was whatever followed the droid crashing through the window they had been peering through moments earlier.

Virgil was sucked in the direction of the breach, but the cell bars between him and the potential of being thrown into outer space acted as a temporary barrier of safety. He made a noise that didn't sound like any language Brandon was familiar with, and the bounty hunter craned his head around the room to see a bunch of other Binarians rush in with weapons.

"Come on!" L3-NY called to the captain, automatically swinging into action. He fired off some shots as his feet hunkered down into the solid floor of the ship while Binarians were thrown here and there by the window breach.

Brandon's legs flailed in part due to the grip of the outside and in part to his desire to kick Virgil in the face, but regardless of the efforts, he couldn't connect.

A short while later, a reinforced shutter of some kind collapsed over the hole in the ship, blocking off the breach. Stability slowly regained its hold on being the norm as equilibrium was reached, which meant that both L3-NY and the remaining Binarians were back on equal footing.

Even if the numbers overwhelmed that of a single trigger-happy droid.

Virgil turned back to Brandon and drew a blade from behind his back.

"Tough luck, Falcon," Virgil said. "I must thank you for indeed being the bait for your ship full of expendables and the dear lost princess of Binary falling right into our clutches. It's just a shame the last thing you're going to see is just one of your crew fall to mine."

"Right. First off…Technically, we have a *Queen* on board, thanks to you," Brandon said. "Second, I think Lenny is doing pretty good on his own…" he said, watching as L3-NY continued to dart around the room, shooting down and holding off the onslaught of enemies. "And thirdly…I'm a long way away from the last thing I'm going to see. But maybe the last thing you're going to see is my foot in your face."

Virgil looked at the distance between himself and the captain and rolled his eyes.

"May I remind you that you're currently tethered to the ceiling?"

Brandon nodded. "That's true. But guess what?"

The bounty hunter pulled himself up, placing his feet up onto the ceiling, the restraints keeping him up via the magnetic locking.

Virgil sighed as he watched the bounty hunter struggle. The Binarian took a single step at a time towards Brandon, blade ready to strike.

But Brandon knew what he was doing. He twisted his arms counter-clockwise at the wrists. Then pushing off the ceiling with his feet, the bounty hunter fell back to the ground. The Binarian was taken aback for a second, which allowed Brandon to roll away from his potential attacker, and hop up onto one knee.

"No hands!"

The bounty hunter raised his arms, and sure enough, he was stating fact. Virgil froze in his place.

"W-what?…"

Brandon smirked and nodded up towards his gauntlets. "I lost a lot of things during the War, but at least I didn't lose my sense of humour."

And with that, he pounced towards the Binarian, still off-guard. Brandon tackled him and the blade scattered away from Virgil, slipping between the bars and into the side of the room where L3-NY continued to fight.

"Hey Falcon!" L3-NY called, ducking behind some cover as his overheated weapon cooled down. "Are you coming?"

Brandon gave Virgil a headbutt before the Binarian kicked him away. "I'm on it!"

The bounty hunter stumbled to his feet before Virgil grabbed his legs and brought him to the floor once again. Regaining the upper hand, the Binarian began to swing blows at Brandon, to which he tried his best to block, raising his arms.

Meanwhile, L3-NY threw a flash grenade that stunned a couple other Binarians, and with a whip around his cover the droid took them out before spinning across to a parallel piece of cover. He threw a micro Black Hole that drew in a few more Binarians alongside all manner of technology around them that struck at their vulnerabilities.

Brandon wriggled free of Virgil's grasp and threw a leg towards the Binarian's chest. The blow was enough to distract him enough to think of a plan of attack in the next few seconds. He spotted the blade. Virgil followed his gaze before looking back to the bounty hunter and his lack of hands. The Binarian smirked. Brandon looked down at his arms.

But that didn't stop him. He bolted towards Virgil and launched off the ground, but this time, his aim wasn't to take down his opponent. It was to merely get past him, and closer towards the Binarian's blade.

The bounty hunter proved to be fast enough. He managed to get past Virgil faster than the Binarian could react. Brandon slid around the ship's floor towards the cell bars and towards the blade. The captain hit the button on his chest to disengage his helmet and opened his mouth to grab the hilt between his teeth.

Then the ship tilted. Something was shooting the ship.

It was the Second Chance.

Of course this was a good sign for Brandon and L3-NY, but the timing couldn't have been worse. The ship's movement threw the blade further away from Brandon's grasp, skittering along the room towards where L3-NY stood.

Virgil took this lucky shot as his opportunity to storm towards Brandon once again. He grabbed the bounty hunter by the shoulders and pulled him towards the cell bars. The Binarian threw Brandon's head against the bars. Brandon avoided a second collision with the bars by redeploying his helmet, but then Virgil grabbed his arms.

The Binarian gripped the captain in a bearhug. Squeezing tighter and tighter, Brandon felt all the air rush out of his body and none coming back to replenish him. He felt dazed and confused as the Binarian took the lead.

L3-NY was still locked in a firefight with the refresh of goons coming into the room, slowly running out of toys to use against them with wave after wave. The droid took a look towards the cell to where Brandon was facing off with Virgil and turned all of his attentions on them for a moment.

He took a shot towards the Binarian in the attempt of making him let go of the captain. Virgil was taken out of his moment of incoming victory in his battle with Brandon by the fire towards him, pulling Brandon away, deeper into the cell.

The moment was just enough for Brandon to regain his hold on the events going down. He snapped to attention and forced his way out of Virgil's grip.

L3-NY didn't spin back towards his aggressors fast enough when the gun he had was shot out of his hand. As well as having his hand shot off his arm.

"Oh come on!" the droid said, before using his other hand to grab at another toy: a good old-fashioned grenade. He pulled out the pin and waited a couple of seconds before throwing it towards the Binarians. It didn't go off on 3. Or 4. Or 5. One of the Binarians rushed to the grenade and picked it up to throw it back.

He got to the picking up stage.

With the rest of that wave of Binarians taken care of, L3-NY looked down at his hand and bent down to reach it. His eyes, however, went instead to the blade beside him.

"Hello there…"

Brandon and Virgil continued their fight. Virgil swung as if he had sharp claws as he brought his offensive, while Brandon threw his body and momentum into kicks in the hope to incapacitate the Binarian that way.

"Falcon!" L3-NY called from outside the cell. The bounty hunter looked over, and noticed the flicker of light reflected of Virgil's blade. The droid looked at Falcon's arms. "Oh hey! Maybe I should lend you a hand!"

L3-NY raised his own arm with its recently shot off hand.

"No thanks, I've already got your leg!" Brandon called, before looking up at his golden gauntlets still attached to the ceiling due to the magnetised restraints.

L3-NY nodded. Virgil didn't take much time to hear any other words come from the bounty hunter or the droid. The Binarian began his attack.

The droid took aim and threw the blade. It was far off target from hitting Virgil, but that was not his target. His plan was that hopefully a Binarian blade could cut through certain materials. Having not come across one in the System until now, it was all down to chance.

It took no time at all for the blade to soar through the air, beyond the bars of the cell Brandon and Virgil stood, and towards Brandon's suspended gauntlets. The bounty hunter took a spin to the side away from Virgil's all-out attack, and under his gauntlets.

L3-NY's gambit paid off, for the Binarian blade did indeed slide through the cuffs holding the gauntlets together and against the ceiling, cutting them open.

Brandon's gauntlets fell towards the floor, where the bounty hunter was ready and waiting. Lined up and ready to go, Brandon twisted his arms clockwise and locked them into position. The captain pivoted and swung his foot around, bringing himself to face Virgil once again.

The Binarian regained his footing and moved himself to face Brandon eye to eye. He took a few steps back as he sized up his opponent.

"Hmm," Virgil said. "Cute trick. But just because you got your shiny gloves back doesn't mean you're going to get out of this alive."

"Oh well," Brandon said, raising his fingers to his mouth and whistling. "It will be all the more impressive when I survive then."

"And your robot friend?"

"Hey!" L3-NY called, stepping towards the cell. The room was lined with the bodies of defeated Binarians. "I'm a droid. Watch your language."

"Is there a difference?" Virgil shrugged and he charged towards Brandon.

The Binarian blade that sat embedded into the ceiling dropped. And straight towards Brandon's opened right hand. With a flourish and a downwards stab, the bounty hunter managed to catch Virgil unexpected.

By slamming the own blade into the Binarian's foot. Virgil screamed in pain as Brandon tried to hush him with his finger.

"Never overestimate your opponent," Brandon said. He gestured towards the cell window. Outside stood the Second Chance. Brandon looked upon his ship once again and smiled. "Turns out only two of us needed to take down your ship. Just imagine what the five of us could do with the rest of you on Binary?"

Virgil gritted his teeth through the pain. "You don't know what you've signed yourself up for!"

"Evidently, I never do," Brandon acknowledged.

The bounty hunter walked over to the window and tapped it. He looked over to L3-NY, who kicked open the cell door, his shot off hand under his armpit.

Brandon looked back to Virgil, who didn't once pull his eyes away from the man who bested him.

"Is this where you kick me in the face? The last thing I'll ever see?"

Brandon moved around to stand above Virgil, looking him into the eyes.

"…No," Brandon said. "This is not that time. I'm sure I'm going to see you again."

"You'll regret this," Virgil said as Brandon made his way out of the cell, following L3-NY.

The bounty hunter turned back to the Binarian as he pulled the cell door closed. Virgil began to grab at the blade to pull it out of his foot.

"Oh, you'll regret doing that," Brandon said. L3-NY raised his gun and shot the cell window as the two of them went deeper into the ship.

"That was badass," L3-NY said as they went looking for Brandon's inventory.

"I know, right? How am I ever going to top that?"

"No, I mean for me," L3-NY said. "Did you see me hold off all those guys?"

"Yeah, with my stuff."

"That you don't even use that much."

"Hey, time and a place," Brandon said as he opened the room where he spotted his Stunderbuss.

The bounty hunter smiled as he made his way inside. The cool electric glow of the room's lighting just highlighted to the captain how special he found his tools. Brandon reached for his trusty sidearm when he spotted the reflection of the light in his gauntlets. He looked to his hands and turned them around. His smile dropped a little, but he stood firm. L3-NY leant over to him.

"You never told me you lost your hands," L3-NY said.

"It wasn't important to know, all things considered."

"Anyone else know?"

"Tia, and that's about it," Brandon said.

The droid nodded. "You're a hero for that day way back when, Falcon."

"It sure doesn't feel like it."

L3-NY patted Brandon on the back. "Well, once we finish this job, you'll see."

"Will I?"

"No. But you'll be so damn rich you could swim in all that money you won't have to feel anything else."

"*Like Ducktales…*"

"Like Ducktales," L3-NY said as a motivated Brandon picked up his Stunderbuss, Electro-Whip, broken hoverboard, and other assorted items. "…Whatever that means."

Chapter Fifteen

In no time at all, Brandon and L3-NY found themselves back on the Second Chance, well on their way through hyperspace away from wherever the Binarians were and nearer to the arranged rendezvous location with the bounty hunters they had met in the Gilded Diamond sympathetic to their cause (and pay-out).

With the two of them in the common room joined by Ceres, Tia, and even Ko'Tex, it was time to get down to business.

"And so I guess we find ourselves where it all began," Brandon said, looking around. "Well, for me. And Ceres. But then came the finding of you three. Again. Since…"

"Wow, you're bad at this," Tia said as she focused on fixing L3-NY's hand.

"It's just…" Brandon scratched the back of his head. "It's been quite the whirlwind timeline. Betrayals, teaming up, that time L3-NY's ship blew up…"

"And to think I almost forgot about that…" L3-NY sighed.

"But," Brandon stood up straight, addressing the others. "What matters is…we have each other."

Ko'Tex gave him a look that confirmed that they weren't exactly on the same boat.

"Well. We at least have the company of fellow bounty hunters, a dangerous criminal, and a princess finding her way home the long way around."

The group looked around and nodded.

"It's a far cry from our days on the other side, L3-NY," Brandon looked to the droid. "Or my training with you, Tia," Brandon nodded to the alien. "Or when L3-NY punched you in the face, Tia…"

"That was not that long ago," Tia said.

"Or," Brandon said, "When I was tasked to bring you back to Binary where those people who killed your family would most likely kill you too, Ceres."

"You really *are* bad at this…" Ceres said, curling her legs up onto her chair.

"The point is…is that…is…"

"Approaching waypoint," Cherry, the Second Chance's A.I. interjected.

"Damnit," Brandon said, turning back towards the door and heading towards the bridge. "Now I have to start this whole speech again."

Brandon sat himself back into his chair as the Second Chance made its way towards the designated meeting place. Far below them orbited the planet of Binary. It was endgame. In a trek that took Brandon and the slowly assembled crew of the Second Chance around various planets and hazards in the System, it was now the final test.

And thankfully, they were not alone.

The bounty hunter nodded and smiled as he scanned the perimeter. Sure enough, the captain found his ship in the presence of dozens of other ships of all different shapes and sizes. Custom jobs, hijacked vessels, even the odd bounty reward or two. Brandon had not only formed a team for the Second Chance and the main motion to make good on their mission, but he had also tempted the ways of the outsiders of System society to unite in a good cause with a great potential pay-out.

It was not long until the Battle for Binary could commence. First, however, the bounty hunter needed to rally his troops composed of seemingly the rest of the System's bounty hunters. It just continued to prove that nothing is a better point of persuasion than money.

Brandon rubbed his hands together and pressed the button on the bridge controls to communicate with the rest of the ships.

"Glad you could all make it," Brandon spoke. To the left of him, Brandon could see the various comms links of the fellow ships opening, giving him visuals of pilots and sound waves of the more secretive of the assembled bounty hunters. The numbers had certainly amassed, and the captain hoped it would be enough for the germ of the plan still spinning in his mind. "Today is a big day for all of us. We are about to save a kingdom, we're about to do more good than the Alliance could have ever done, we're about to – "

Before Brandon could continue a speech that would no-doubt slowly turn into a disaster, one of the distant ships blew up. Not on its own, Brandon knew that almost instantaneously. Being that near to Binary and the knowledge that he himself and his crew that included the Lost Queen of Binary Fields were still alive, it wasn't too far a stretch to consider that the usurper Binarians were going to strike as soon as they could. Especially once they realise that the loitering ships just outside their airspace were about to get a little too close for comfort.

Brandon pushed another button to project his voice throughout the Second Chance. "All hands to battle stations. All hands to battle stations."

A few moments later the others gathered inside to join Brandon. Ceres took the seat next to the captain; L3-NY took his seat at the weapons controls; Tia took the seat next to the droid; and Ko'Tex preferred to stand, rubbing his claws together.

The captain took a moment to look around him. It had been too long since the Second Chance had a full crew on board manning the various stations. Brandon hadn't needed to man half of them most of the time, but seeing as this was about to be a raging battle to put the ship through its paces, he was glad he put together a group of people who could help out.

"Right," Brandon said to his crew, before turning back to the controls, switching things to fully manual. "In the words of the great *Darkwing Duck*…Let's. Get. Dangerous."

A beat of silence filled the room until Ceres spoke up.

"Who?"

"Come on, princess," Brandon's head lowered. "We've been over this, watch the darn cartoons, jeez…"

A few button presses and switch flicking over continued annoyed muttering later and the Second Chance swung its way into the fray.

Brandon piloted his ship with as much ease as he could as the bounty hunters and the Binarians began their battle in space above Binary. It was no-longer a case of one solitary ship trying to escape the pursuit of the Binarian fleet, but now it seemed that a mismatched collection of ships great and small formed a solid foil to the drone-like formations of the Binarians.

The Second Chance barrel-rolled and loop-de-looped its way around gunfire. Its shields were fully operational and maintained by Ceres while L3-NY took his hand at the weapons.

"Silly question, but rules of engagement?" L3-NY asked, slipping into his old ways.

"Rules of engagement are shoot anything that looks like its about to shoot us."

"You don't have to tell me twice," L3-NY acknowledged, and began to use the ships beam weapons. Brandon raised a hand.

"But keep collateral damage and casualties to a minimum," the captain instructed.

Ko'Tex sneered and spat. "Cowardly little Falcon..."

Brandon continued to manoeuvre the Second Chance around impossible angles that resulted in the nearest of misses between Binarian and bounty hunter ship alike.

"Ko'Tex I understand your bloodlust, but just because these guys have tried to kill us doesn't mean we should go out of our way to try and kill them back," Brandon explained as he pulled up to avoid the slow pincer movement of a couple of Binarian ships. "If anything, they are more guilty of being cowards in every choice they've made in their want to kill the princess."

Ko'Tex shook his head and looked across the battlefield. "Your hesitation to actually do something will be your downfall."

"Yeah, well, there's a reason you're such a wanted fugitive and I get to be the one to bring you in."

"We shall see once we have our rematch."

Brandon rolled his eyes before rolling the Second Chance out of the way of a missile strike.

L3-NY's hands were a blur as he implemented every trick available to him to get the most out of the Second Chance's weapons. The system wasn't as streamlined as the original Alliance systems the once-Grasshopper-Class had, but the droid continued to work his magic.

"Tia, can I get more power to these cannons?" L3-NY asked above the sound of his clattering fingers.

"If I do we'll be risking the shield integrity," Tia said as she continued to monitor and manipulate the systems.

"Do it," Brandon said, his tongue sticking out of his mouth in concentration.

Ceres' eyes darted all around the monitors as the Second Chance returned fire and tried its best to avoid any serious damage. The princess placed her hands on the ship console and through her technopathy she found ways to hold the Second Chance together a little better. She could sense in the patchwork that was Brandon's modifications of the Second Chance that some of the seams were being pulled apart in the motions.

It wasn't a surprise given the previous troubles the ship had had since she first came aboard, but things were just a little bit more intense that time around. Ceres tried her best to close vents and otherwise manipulate parts of the ship directly, rather than indirectly controlling them at a slower pace due to having to do so via the ship's computers.

"Um," Ceres said. "I may have jettisoned some of the cargo from the Black Hole smuggling bays."

"What?" Brandon said, only half-concentrating on his side of the conversation as he whipped the Second Chance around into a better firing position for L3-NY. "Aw man, there was stuff in there I still needed to sell…"

"If it helps, that stuff seems to be doing a good job colliding with passing Binarian ships," Tia noted with a quick gaze out the window.

Ko'Tex flexed and flicked his arms, the claws coming out the back of his hands itching for some combat.

"When are we going to clash blades with these 'Binarians' for real?" Ko'Tex said.

"Well hopefully the bounty hunters will have already taken care of most of them," Brandon said, rolling the Second Chance one direction and then soon another, the bridge rotating on gyroscopes in order to keep in a stable position. All around the captain's ship other crafts were blowing up or retreating. From both sides of the conflict. Being brave and stupid went hand in hand, and that wasn't truer than with the bounty hunters of the Gilded Diamond. The chase for just one more bounty drove many towards going the extra mile.

It was something Brandon found admirable in his kin. But also something that injected sorrow in his actions, for they signed up on a dangerous mission on the word and promises of Brandon. The bounty hunter always had a strange attitude towards death and the way he dealt with it, and by all rights, he probably would have been more suited for a less hazardous profession, especially with his particular set of morals, but in that moment of doubt he had had many times before, his eyes flicked away from everything else going on around him and found solace in the stars.

And for that moment he filled with a warmth and optimism and motivation he always felt when he looked to the System in all its beauty. Brandon would travel through the gates of Hell if it meant he could continue to travel the System.

But then he saw a sight that became his gates of Hell. Many more ships began to break the sight of the stars from where Brandon sat. New crafts joined the fray, but they weren't more bounty hunters to help or more Binarians to back-up the seemingly endless wave of defenders.

It was the Alliance.

"Oh no," Brandon said as he noticed the approaching formation. "Oh no, not now…"

Ceres couldn't help but look over to Brandon as he began to lose his composure. In all honesty the crew all had the feeling that they were already up against insurmountable odds let alone having the Alliance join the conflict.

The Alliance began to blare across all frequencies.

"By the power given by the Treaty, we – The Alliance – order you to stand down from this act of war."

"This isn't a war," Brandon muttered, avoiding the usage of the communications. "We're doing a better justice that what you've ever done."

Ceres put a hand on Brandon's shoulder.

"Please don't do anything stupid," the princess said.

"Don't worry, I'm not exactly going to leap into a full-on fight with the Alliance," Brandon said. "Not again."

Ko'Tex, on the other hand, was more than ready for a fight. He laughed and raised his arms.

"Haha!" the Selenian called. "Now I'm ready to fight! Come on you Alliance dogs! Try to fight me!"

"God, you really like calling them 'Alliance Dogs', don't you?" Brandon shook his head.

"Beam them aboard!" Ko'Tex gestured to Brandon, ignoring the bounty hunter's disapproval.

"I…you can't just beam someone aboard! That's impossible!" Brandon said.

"The amount of stuff you've seen and you think teleportation isn't possible?" Ceres questioned.

"Wait, does that mean you Binarians know how to teleport?"

Ceres paused.

"No, but…"

The door to the bridge opened, drawing everyone's attention.

And Virgil stepped inside.

"*Falcon.*"

Brandon's eyes widened and pushed back into his seat, his attentions locked on the trespassing Binarian. The captain didn't even notice the ships outside disobeying the orders of the Alliance that had surrounded them, engaging in a three-way combat between the recruited bounty hunters, the Binarian ships, and the Alliance.

The bounty hunter pointed at the intruder.

"T-Teleportation!" Brandon said. "You *can* do it!"

Virgil's visage began to flicker and flash. Even jitter. Something was not quite right. Ceres began to speak.

"We haven't discovered a way on Binary to teleport. But he isn't from Binary."

The Binarian began to twitch and shake his head unnaturally. It was not behaviour that Brandon expected from Virgil. He hadn't even considered that Virgil would be found anywhere near Binary having been left stranded on a ship at Brandon's unwillingness to put a stop to him completely.

"None of them are," Ceres said.

Virgil's face began to break into a mosaic of patches of skin that slowly flipped and rotated. His appearance began to shift from the humanoid appearance Brandon knew him as. The race of which Ceres resembled. Virgil slowly gained the appearance of something a lot more sinister and imposing.

"They…are Viruses."

In the doorway – more than a foot taller than his original form – stood Virgil. Now jet black and scaly. Serpentine eyes that flittered, a rich blue tongue flicked around pointed fangs, hands that ended with three claws to rival that of Ko'Tex.

"Okay…" Brandon said, his eyes incapable to tearing away from the evolving horror before them.

Virgil's back cracked and snapped into position, rolling his shoulders and flashing his razor-sharp claws. Hissing replaced all communication that came from him. Whatever humanity was there was long-since gone. If it ever existed in the first place.

"…Is there anything else you haven't been telling us, Ceres?" Brandon asked.

"Yeah, because this seems quite up there on the need for full disclosure list!" L3-NY said.

Both Brandon and L3-NY reached for their weapons and took shots at Virgil. The creature didn't even react. Its hide negated the shots, absorbing them.

Ceres quickly turned her back on Virgil and placed her hands on the console. Without any warning, the door of the bridge came slamming down on the curved back of the creature. The force was strong, but not enough to completely damage Virgil. It did serve well enough to momentarily distract the Virus, creating the need for Virgil to force the heavy door off its body.

Ko'Tex snarled and charged towards Virgil, tackling the Virus out of the bridge, the door completely slamming down behind them. Brandon took that moment to swing himself back towards the battle outside the Second Chance and weighed up the bigger situation.

"Great," Brandon said, his eyes darting across the console and the various readouts Cherry generated. His hands went back to the controls and narrowly pulled away from a stray shot in their direction.

The others went back to their respective jobs, still distracted by the battle closer to home.

"Cherry, run surveillance footage," Brandon called.

"Affirmative," Cherry said, before producing live streams of each of the surveillance cameras across the Second Chance.

The camera right outside the bridge picked up the action. Selenian and Virus locking claws.

"What…what even is that?" Brandon said, looking back and forth between piloting his ship and the footage.

"A Virus," Ceres said as they watched Ko'Tex jump and dodge away from Virgil's slashes. "The true form of the people who ravaged my home."

"Like a computer virus?" L3-NY asked, running his finger across the missile controls to release a barrage of weaponry.

"It's just the name we call them," Ceres said with a shake of the head. As she watched the fight going on from the other side of the door, she began using her technopathy to manipulate valves that blew scalding steam towards Virgil, offering openings for Ko'Tex to strike. "For they corrupt and destroy from within. Without discrimination. They just do what they do to survive and grow. Usually across the backs of innocents."

Brandon's eyes noticed Virgil grasping Ko'Tex around the neck, his free hand about to stab into the Selenian's stomach with his clawed hands. Ko'Tex proved to still have some fight in him.

"This isn't good," the captain noted. He went back to throwing himself into piloting the Second Chance. The battle above Binary continued to rage. The Alliance and the Binarians continued to have the upper hand, the allies of the Second Chance slowly dwindling. Brandon noticed that many were not destroyed but merely fled, which was something the bounty hunter could sympathise with. On a different day he may have considered doing the same, but this was it. The best opportunity they would have to come out on top. Even if that meant facing off against both the Alliance and the Binarians at the peak of their space-fleet capability.

"Lenny," Brandon said. "Do you have any worms?"

"I'm pretty sure this whole battle is phasing you, captain, so you might have forgotten…" L3-NY said, recharging the Second Chance's beams. "…That I am a droid."

"I mean to infect enemy technology, do you have any?"

"Of course," L3-NY said. He flipped open a flap on his chest and pulled out a small device. "But there's too many ships, I don't have enough to take down all these guys."

"Well," Brandon said, pulling up on the controls to drastically raise the Second Chance. Outside the bridge, Ko'Tex and Virgil rolled further back into the ship. "I don't want you to use the worms on those enemy ships."

The captain pressed a few buttons on his console and then got out of his seat, the ship's autopilot engaging.

"I want you to use it on that," he said, pointing down to Binary.

Ceres nodded. "The holo-dome."

"You want me to use a worm to take down an entire holo-dome?" L3-NY asked.

"Can you do it?"

"Can a spillage of toxic waste create a group of adolescent anthropomorphic reptiles that are adept at hand-to-hand combat and eating junk food?"

Brandon's face lit up.

"YES. I mean, it can't really…unfortunately…but yes, Lenny! That's exactly what I want to hear!"

"Yeah!" L3-NY said, pulling out multiple devices containing deployable worms. "Like *Sewer Sharks*!"

Brandon's feeling of being impressed by L3-NY soon dissipated.

"Okay, seriously, if we get out of this alive we're all going to have some cartoon time," Brandon said, before drawing his Electro-Whip and leaving the bridge.

"Our fearless leader," Tia observed.

With the Second Chance's autopilot flying the ship towards Binary and L3-NY working on bringing down the protective holo-dome over the kingdom, Brandon momentarily left his crew to hold the bridge as he went in search of Ko'Tex and Virgil.

It was not too hard to do, all he had to do is follow the ravaged corridors where claws had sliced through metal and bodies had crashed into walls.

Brandon swung the Electro-Whip in small circles, his movement silent all except for the low hum of the weapon in his hand. While up close and personal didn't seem to be the best option having seen the true form of Virgil, the Electro-Whip still offered Brandon options.

Nothing was immune to the whip's voltage. It packed a hell of a sting, certainly enough to constrict the movements of a murderous jet-black creature.

The deeper he trekked into the bowels of the ship, the more came apparent that Ko'Tex and Virgil were locked in an even battle. Collateral damage was abounding, and the strange colours of two sets of blood denoted that neither side really wanted to back down.

Something crunched under Brandon's foot. It was glass. The bounty hunter looked up and saw the shattered bulb above him before the sound of grunts and solid bodies hitting unstable walls of the ship drew the bounty hunter's attention.

Cautious, the captain tiptoed his way further towards the back of the ship, where the fully constructed nature of the ship soon gave way to the unfinished pipes and grating. Brandon contemplated for a moment the things he could do with the rest of his ship once this bounty was completed. If it were ever to be completed. For one thing, he'd try and make the least reliable area of the ship – the stuff that actually makes the ship a ship – less of a death trap.

As he rounded the corner, Brandon watched as Ko'Tex swung his right claw towards Virgil, nicking his arm and spilling blood across the wall. Part of him thought it was about to burn right through it with acid, but instead it just clung to it. No doubt it was going to stain.

Brandon moved around to a better position as the fight continued, noticing that the actual form of Virgil also sported clawed feet as well as the hands. All appendages of violence and danger. The bounty hunter continued his hesitant stride as he weighed up the situation. As Ko'Tex seemed to gain ground, Brandon reached for his holster and drew his revolver. It was rather dangerous to shoot rounds in the direction of the two in battle in case a bullet made contact with ally rather than foe, but the captain knew what he was aiming at.

Virgil flung a kick against Ko'Tex, knocking the Selenian away and deeper into the half-finished passageways. The clattering echoed around the Second Chance as Brandon took steps closer towards the conflict, gun drawn. With his eye on the prize, Brandon aimed and fired.

Virgil's attention was pulled from Ko'Tex at the sound of the sudden gunshot and the rushing stream of steam that flew out of the nearby pierced pipe. Brandon had no idea what that particular pipe connected to or whether it would affect the path the Second Chance flew on, but he knew it was one way to keep the Virus at bay.

The Electro-Whip uncoiled, Brandon swung and lashed the melee weapon as he progressed towards Virgil. Ko'Tex kept his eyes on the enemy, but he didn't rush ahead. It didn't help that the steam impeding his initial path had no sign of stopping.

"So, you're a lot uglier than you first made out to be," Brandon taunted. Foot followed foot across the metal grates along the floor. Trying to hold the upper hand would most certainly fail if he tripped. "But come on Virgil, let's make this a fair fight. You seem to be able to hold your own. Lets make this interesting."

He spun his revolver away and holstered it. Clenching his fist and with Electro-Whip in hand, Brandon shrugged and welcomed a fistfight with the antagonist.

And Virgil obliged.

The Virus hissed and moved towards the bounty hunter with haste, each step's sound bouncing around the acoustics of the Second Chance's metallic interior. Brandon hunkered down and took the first blow, flinging him back where he came from, smacking into a nearby wall.

All of the air rushed out of the bounty hunter's lungs as he stumbled in his attempts to get up. This version of Virgil was a lot different to the one he had escaped from.

"Why aren't you always in this form?..." Brandon muttered as he pulled himself up onto his knees. Virgil grabbed the captain's neck and threw him back upright onto his feet. The Virus slashed towards a hurried counter from Brandon's Electro-Whip brandishing. A crack of electricity halted the attempted swipe, which Ko'Tex took as an opening to manoeuvre himself around the steam and towards the battling duo.

Brandon swung a punch that full on connected with Ko'Tex's jaw, but didn't do any damage. The dull thud of metal on the Virus' hide filled the air, followed by the sounds uttered by the bounty hunter when the Virus slashed him.

Ko'Tex tackled Virgil as Brandon tended to the newly formed cuts across his arm. It wasn't too deep, but the captain hesitated to provoke a potential improvement on that bad situation. He wheeled around towards the Selenian clambering on top of the Virus, slashing it a couple times with his own claws.

The Selenian flew through the air as Virgil's defensive swing made contact, the strength of the Virus being enough to ward off the fugitive's aggression.

Brandon moved to replace his ally in the fray once more, but he too was struck by Virgil and again saw himself rapidly accelerating towards the wall before becoming a heap on the ground.

He hit inspiration when he unclenched his eyelids and spotted the grated floor that ran along the makeshift battlefield. With a look towards Virgil, he formed a quick plan of attack. Or rather, defence. The bounty hunter rolled towards the Virus but did not attempt to stand up. Instead he made a gambit on how Virgil would capitalise on the situation.

And it paid off.

The Virus growled and raised its leg; all with the intent to slam down it its razor-sharp claws to impale the poor bounty hunter. Something Brandon hoped Virgil would do. With the positioning of the Virus' claws and the speed of which the downward stab was, Brandon knew that if he just rolled out of the way, the claw would find a neat way into the grating and get momentarily stuck.

Which is exactly what happened. Missing the bounty hunter, the forked, razor-clawed foot of the Virus instead found its way into the grates underfoot. With such a force and in such a position that for a few seconds it would be unable to move much in any direction, Brandon struck back.

Having hopped back onto his feet and with Electro-Whip in hand, Brandon flicked his wrist and the unfurled whip wrapped around the neck of the distracted Virgil. As the volts surged, Brandon yanked forwards, pulling the Virus' head towards him. Yet another lacklustre punch made contact, but it was still enough to annoy Virgil.

As he pulled back the Electro-Whip, Brandon took another step back. It was advantageous in that situation to judge distance lest another claw swing in retaliation slice open vital arteries or worse. Ko'Tex on the other hand, didn't share the sentiment, and began to rush forwards once again.

Brandon spun 180 degrees and raised his arms, catching Ko'Tex as he charged ahead. The bounty hunter was surprised that that collision didn't knock himself clean off his feet as he pushed back against the Selenian to hold their ground.

Virgil hissed and struggled to remove its foot from the floor, flailing its arms, hoping one of his two opponents were stupid enough to get so close again. The Virus eventually did pull its foot free, but not without pulling up the grating with it opening a pretty large hole to the floor below.

The bounty hunter smiled and swung the Electro-Whip again, the crackle of electricity shocking and surging as it curled around Virgil's other foot. Brandon pulled the handle of the whip with sharp force, throwing the Virus towards the captain and the Selenian.

And the hole between the three of them.

Virgil stumbled off-balance before falling down the hole, the metal grating stuck between his claws coming off as it struck against the floor. It wasn't the end for the Virus but it was certainly a setback. Brandon looked to Ko'Tex.

"You better get to the bridge."

Ko'Tex didn't budge. "Why, Falcon?!"

Brandon pulled away the grating and peered down towards the lower part of the ship.

"Because if you stay here when I kick this stowaway off my ship without a suit on, I'm pretty sure the change in pressure isn't going to agree with you," he said, before hopping down after Virgil. He shouted back up to Ko'Tex. "Like, you're going to explode! Or something…"

Ko'Tex's eyes bulged as he heard that.

Brandon looked around the darkened interior of the Second Chance, trying to find where Virgil went. The bounty hunter clapped his hands to turn the lights on, and a second after that a humanoid Virgil tackled him.

The bounty hunter swung a headbutt towards Virgil and hit him right on the forehead. The Virus stumbled back, clutching his face as Brandon returned to a fighting stance.

"Wearing a mask again, I see," Brandon said.

"You're only postponing defeat, *Falcon*," Virgil said, his voice more electronic.

"Is what I say to you," Brandon said, forming a fist. "If your name was Falcon."

The two of them both swung for the other, both fists connecting with the other's face. They pulled their arms back. Brandon shook the pain off.

"So you're all just a bunch of shapeshifter-y aliens," Brandon said, rubbing his face as it felt many pinpricks. "Just a disease spreading throughout the universe."

"We are not a disease, we are – "

Brandon threw a finger towards Virgil. "Do not say it! Do not say you are the cure!"

Virgil hesitated.

"I…I wasn't going to say that!"

Silence.

"You totally were!"

"I…"

The Virus sounded unimpressed.

"Knew it!"

Virgil stood confidently across from the bounty hunter.

"Well, Falcon, you can live in the solace of that small victory being your last."

"Oh yeah?" Brandon said, raising his other fist clenching the Electro-Whip.

"Yeah," Virgil said, raising his fist, revealing that he now held Brandon's Electro-Whip. The bounty hunter looked down at his empty hands.

"First you, then your crew, then the princess," Virgil nodded as he moved forwards, swinging the whip.

Brandon rolled and dodged from the Electro-Whip as best as he could. All around him sparks and jolts of electricity scattered. Near misses became a little too near. The bounty hunter howled in pain when the whip's aim was true and Brandon felt a dose of his own medicine. He tensed and rolled against the ground and clutched at muscles contracting at the contact of the blows.

Virgil enjoyed the advantage he had as Brandon looked up towards the ceiling they had fallen from. A solid block of light shone from above through the hole in the grating. The bounty hunter wished he didn't instruct Ko'Tex to get back to the cockpit as soon as he did. He was now on the back foot, and Virgil was upon him. Brandon looked around and noticed what he needed.

The captain found his way back onto his feet, still reeling from the shocks he received. The Virus showed no signs of stopping so Brandon had to see if he could bring an end to things. He ran to the side of Virgil, just narrowly avoiding a swing of the Electro-Whip aimed towards his neck. Brandon stumbled, but fell in the direction he needed to go: the release of the nearby bay doors.

Brandon pushed it with force and breathed a sigh of relief for the victory before the suction of space outside tugged on his back. The bounty hunter slammed his chest and deployed his helmet as he grabbed onto a nearby column to steady himself. He turned and grinned in the knowledge that Virgil was surely to become a victim of his quick thinking, but alas that was not to be the case.

Virgil swung the Electro-Whip as he too was pulled towards the opening bay doors. Somehow, he managed to get it around a parallel pillar to the one Brandon clung to. Brandon watched as the Virus was unshaken by the pressure changes. A flashing red light drew his attention away, noticing the indication that the bay doors were stuck. Far from open, but not exactly closed, either.

The flailing of their legs began to subside as space sped by outside the Second Chance. They were no doubt getting closer to Binary's surface by Brandon's reckoning, and as the pressure had began to equalise time was running out. Without Virgil taken care of there would still be one very pesky Virus alongside however many Virus were out there between getting Ceres back to her birth right.

Brandon and Virgil found themselves back on their feet as the Second Chance levelled out. Virgil laughed.

"So much for your plan, Falcon," he said.

"Yeah, I was hoping for it to be a little more successful…" Brandon said, eyes darting around.

There was nothing else in the room to help him, but he still checked his pockets for anything he could use. Then he felt something. The bounty hunter pulled it out, revealing a sphere.

Virgil hesitated for a moment, then determined it wasn't an explosive or similar device. Brandon pulled back and threw it towards the Virus, to which Virgil made no real effort to avoid the poor aim. He tutted.

"Oh, Brandon, what's happened to your aim?"

"Nothing," the bounty hunter replied, and clenched his fist. The sphere shot back towards Brandon's hand, slamming into the back of Virgil's head along the way.

The captain caught the sphere and stepped towards the stumbling Virgil. His other hand took a hold of the Electro-Whip's handle and disengaged it, spinning around the side of the Virus and throwing him over his hip. The Virus flipped in the air and rolled a couple times before pulling himself back up, and by that point, Brandon was ready.

And he smiled.

Virgil laughed as he looked at his position – his back towards the gap between the open bay doors.

"So I guess this is your final move, Falcon?" Virgil said, no effort to move. "Where the last thing I'll see is 'your foot in my face'?…"

Brandon paused for a moment.

Virgil continued to provoke the bounty hunter's attack. "And you'll kick me out of your ship and will no doubt bring an end to your whole stupid attitude of not kill – "

A metal leg swung through the air and kicked Virgil in the chest. He screamed as he rolled backwards and out of the bay doors.

L3-NY put his foot back on the ground, taking the option to pose. "That's for shooting my hand off."

"He wasn't the one who shot your hand off," Brandon said, sighing with relief.

"Yeah, well," L3-NY scratched the back of his head despite the fact he couldn't feel it. "It seems cooler if you pretend he did before I did that."

Brandon shook his head and looked to L3-NY and then over to Ko'Tex, who wore a suit that looked a size or two small for him.

"My heroes," Brandon said. He looked over to the bay doors and the flashing light. "Those doors are jammed. Need them closed if we wanna land in one piece."

Ko'Tex nodded and moved over to the doors. With ease, he gripped them and pulled them shut.

"Wow, this Selenian is pretty strong, maybe *he* should've kicked that dude out of the ship," L3-NY observed.

"Don't worry, he'll have his chance to shine soon enough," Brandon pat Ko'Tex on the back. "How's the whole 'Getting onto Binary' plan going?"

"Well, we got the holo-dome down…"

"That's good."

"But the air defences are still up."

"That's bad."

"We tweaked our course, though, so we'll be heading just outside to the 'Binary Fields' as Ceres called them and we'll be out of range. Just."

"That's good," Brandon nodded. "Wait, who touched the Second Chance's flight controls?"

"I did."

Brandon looked to L3-NY, displeased.

"The Second Chance is my ship to pilot, that was bad!"

"What if you're not around and we need to fly this bucket of bolts?"

"If I died or something, you mean?" Brandon said. "Nothing. You wouldn't be able to do anything, the Second Chance is wired so if I die, the Second Chance self-destructs."

"…Really?"

"No. But if we get out of this alive, remind me to install that feature. In fact…" Brandon gestured for L3-NY and Ko'Tex to follow him back to the bridge. "Cherry: Remind me to install a self-destruct feature on the Second Chance in the event of my death."

"Are you sure that's a good idea?" Cherry, the Second Chance's A.I. said.

"It's a *great* idea, what could go wrong?"

Chapter Sixteen

Binary looked darker than Brandon recalled it looking. It wasn't fire and brimstone, but the bounty hunter spied how corrupted the city in the distance had gotten as the Second Chance made a safe landing on the Binary Fields.

The immaculate city appeared to have veins of darkness spreading outwards from its centre. Strikes of the Virus' influence could be seen slowly engulfing the land, and it seemed as if they had come at the best time.

"Seems like we came at the best time!" Brandon called to the others as the exit ramp lowered.

"What have they done?…" Ceres observed, eyes peering outside the window.

"Whatever it is, it's not good," Tia noted, checking her sniper rifle.

"Hey Falcon, you wanna have a bet on who tags more bad guys?" L3-NY asked, spinning his gun.

"No thanks," Brandon said, passing cubes to each of them. "I'm sure Ko'Tex doesn't have any qualms with a gentlemen's wager."

The Selenian looked at the cube in his hand. "What is this? I don't need this."

Brandon took the cube back and waved. "Hoverboards. For all of us. Quickest and stealthiest way into this place. Easy in, easy out."

"I don't think it's going to be easy anywhere," Tia said.

"Hey," Brandon said, turning to the alien. "It'll be easy as a team. We've got a skilled marksman; a walking, talking supercomputer; a super-strong warrior; the technopathic princess who knows this land like the back of her hand; and the cool, intelligent, charming, handsome, awesome, brilliant – "

"Finish your point," Tia said.

"…Me."

"Yeah. Those adjectives totally describe you," L3-NY said.

"Aww, thanks Lenny."

"I was being sar–…Never mind. Just tell us the plan."

"Okay! Well…"

After Brandon explained the plan, the group began their assault of the kingdom of Binary. The call was for as stealthy and sneaky as possible, but to always stay cautious of what hid behind the next corner. All five of them left the Second Chance on Brandon's order. Four took their respective hoverboards as transport, while Ko'Tex decided to continue on foot.

"Seriously, Ko'Tex?" Brandon spoke into his headset. "You realise how far away we are?"

"I don't need your childish vehicles," Ko'Tex said over the communications. "You need to stop underestimating me, Falcon."

"Well you need to stop undermining me, I'm your captain!"

"You wish, Falcon," Ko'Tex laughed. A rare occurrence to Brandon's reckoning. "I am here for the fight. And I am here for the money."

"Well that's not very nice, the others aren't here just because of that," Brandon said, swaying his hoverboard around as the city got closer and closer.

"You say that…" L3-NY began.

"Come on, guys!" Brandon said. "We're here to help Ceres!"

"Don't worry, Brandon," Tia said. "We're all people of our word. We've come to liberate a kingdom and reinstate the rightful heir and stop the corruption of this planet."

"That's right, Tia. Honour among thieves," Brandon nodded and looked over to Tia following Ceres' lead. The four-armed alien wasn't quite as graceful on a hoverboard as she normally was, but the princess was quite the natural. Though Brandon reasoned that was probably due to her technopathy. Then again, he still didn't quite understand the full extent of her abilities.

"You say honour among thieves like it's your catchphrase," L3-NY mused.

"I've said it like three times, it's not my catchphrase!" Brandon replied. "Though I totally *should* have a catchphrase now that you mention it…"

"Guys," Ceres said, turning her head back to look at the others, noticing that Ko'Tex actually wasn't all that too far behind. "Welcome to Binary."

Brandon checked his Stunderbuss and patted around for his other gadgets before looking ahead to the final straight of their collective bounty. "*Fantastico*," he said.

The streets of Binary strewn and coiled around the centre of the kingdom would be labyrinthine and too extensive to explore and navigate without assistance, but with Ceres at the helm they continued their journey at record pace.

"Aren't princesses just locked in towers all their lives?" L3-NY said. "How do you even know this place this well?"

"Well, you know, I was bored of being locked away at home," Ceres answered, hopping and swinging her hoverboard around obstacles. "And all I wanted to do was escape and explore Binary and see how people really lived, so that's what I did. I'd escape, and somehow, Xander would always find me."

"Who's Xander?" L3-NY asked.

"A Knight of the Kingdom of Binary," Brandon answered for Ceres. "I didn't know him long, but I knew he was a man to be trusted. Had his heart in the right place. And I made the promise to finish where he left off."

"After the persuasion of money," Ceres teased.

"Yeah, well," Brandon shrugged, ducking his head to avoid a low-hanging sign. "Okay, looks like we all like the sound of money."

"And violence!" L3-NY said.

"And literally saving a world," Tia said.

"And violence," Ko'Tex said.

"And we also…like money," Brandon nodded.

Ceres laughed. "I'm true to my word. You help me fix this, you shall be rewarded greatly."

"So let's do this!" Brandon called to action. "Tia, we need your sharpshooter abilities as the eye in the sky."

Ceres pointed over to a tower. "Over there! While I wasn't one for being locked up in a tower I do know that's the tallest tower in all of Binary."

"Gotcha," Tia nodded and pulled back the lever on her sniper rifle. She swung her other arms around to help swerve her hoverboard towards the direction of the tower.

"Cool," Brandon clapped his hands together as he, Ceres, and L3-NY powered they way through, getting closer and closer to the castle grounds.

On the rounding of the corner they saw it wasn't as smooth sailing as they thought. While the crew of the Second Chance did well enough to get to that point undetected, it was only a matter of time until they came across the Virus. They were prepared for that moment regardless.

"L3-NY," Brandon nodded. "This is your time to shine."

If the droid had more ability to emote through his face, it would probably show a look of joy and elation as he took his gun in both hands and pulled them apart, creating two working halves.

"Thank you, Brandon," L3-NY whispered. A crack in his voice emulated the droid's voice breaking. "Thank you."

And with that, L3-NY yelled out a loud "Whoo!" before swooping his hoverboard away from the group and towards the advancing Virus troops. Brandon noted that they still remained in their Binarian forms, which meant that Virgil probably didn't have the chance to pass the memo.

Shame he didn't have the chance to before L3-NY kicked him off a spaceship, Brandon thought to himself.

The bounty hunter watched as the droid continued on a gleeful spree of attacking the Virus forces. Wielding his guns akimbo, L3-NY laughed a little too much as he struck down wave after wave, dipping here and there as he avoided incoming fire.

L3-NY took the fair share of gunfire from the Virus, shots ricocheting off his body and into nearby walls. Brandon and Ceres took advantage of the diversion by speeding around the conflict and towards the castle grounds.

The sound of an explosion threw them off for a second. A hurried look over their shoulder revealed that L3-NY was still in one piece, but the hoverboard was not. The droid had ditched the destroyed vehicle and continued his attack on foot.

"Come on, Lenny," Brandon said as he and the Princess approached the guarded castle gate. "I'm running out of hoverboards…"

"Why do you even have this many?" Ceres asked.

"Everyone has to collect *something* in the System," Brandon answered.

"Seems like *I'm* collecting greedy mercenaries…" Ceres muttered.

"Hey!" Brandon raised a finger. "Bounty hunters! Don't use the 'm' word!"

Brandon aimed his Stunderbuss and struck the two guards either side of the gate before they even knew what was happening.

"Mercenaries, I mean. If you thought I meant money…No. Keep saying money."

The bounty hunter and the princess leapt off their hoverboards as they folded back into cubes. Brandon swept them up and stowed them as they began to make a break for the castle steps.

"Lenny!" Brandon spoke into his headset. "How are you doing?"

"Well," the droid said in-between shots heard over from his side. "I would say I was doing good!…But then they blew up the hoverboard and grew like ten times their numbers, so now I'm doing not so good."

"Good thing you're a droid who can be rebuilt," Brandon said.

"I swear, you better give me my leg back after all of this."

"You'll be *fine*," Brandon waved away as he began to climb the steps, Ceres at his side.

Over the other side of the comms Brandon could hear more gunfights and explosions and not a lot else coming from L3-NY.

"Yeah, he'll be fine," Brandon said, disconnecting.

The bounty hunter wasn't ready to face the Virus troops that burst out of the castle doors. Thankfully, someone else was. In quick succession the troops flung backwards from the impact of sniper rounds, followed by the echoed gunshot crack that reverberated around the grounds of Binary Castle.

Brandon and Ceres turned and waved towards the tower in the distance. They weren't sure what level Tia was on, they just knew that wherever she was, she was deadly at that height and range.

"Nice shooting, Tia!" Brandon spoke into his microphone.

"You might have to be on your own in a moment," Tia said, the sound of her pistol filling the halls of the floor she was on. "These Virus guys were already in the building when I got there. And they've got explos– "

Immediately after hearing that, Brandon and Ceres watched helplessly as an explosion filled the entire top floor of the tower. Almost frozen where they stood, Brandon spoke into his headset.

"Tia? Tia? Are you still there?" Brandon spoke into his headset. "Tia?!"

All the captain could hear was static.

"We need to end this," Ceres said, taking initiative. She spun towards the castle doors. They looked secured.

"I'm with you all of the way," Brandon said. He looked over the closer-off entrance. "How do we get inside? Backdoor? Window? Explosives? Knock?"

Ceres smirked. "Don't worry. I still have the key."

She raised her arms and threw them either side of her. The doors flung open, revealing a line of Virus behind it. Brandon jumped straight into action, pulling out a micro Black Hole and throwing it towards the gathered troops. Without fail all of them were sucked towards it. Unable to separate and attack, the bundle of incapacitated Virus made for a safe passage for Brandon and Ceres to skip past.

"Okay," Brandon said, looking back to the open doors and the constricted Virus welcoming party. "That was pretty cool."

"Welcome home," Ceres said. She touched the dark wall and suddenly it shone brightly. With a flick of her wrist, every door along the corridor opened.

"And why did you need me to help you get back home again?" Brandon asked, before being given the answer in the Virus troops that began to flood out of every other door.

"Because I can't fight!" Ceres shouted over the gunfire that began.

"Sure you can!" Brandon said, raising his Stunderbuss. The bounty hunter reached into his back pocket and raised a small silver oblong device. The Virus looked at it and paused, curious to what weaponry the captain had in his hand. "Here's some motivation."

The bounty hunter pressed a button and threw the device up towards the ceiling. It latched onto it and all of the Virus' eyes followed it. Nothing happened for a moment. And then something did. Ceres didn't take long to respond.

"Seriously? You brought music?"

"Yeah!" Brandon said as the unimpressed Virus began to charge. "I felt like this part needed a soundtrack!"

"I'd be a little more excited if you brought something to help stop these guys instead of…"

"BRANDON FALCON!!!" Brandon's singing voice began to blast out of the device on the ceiling. "Hunter of the bounty and the leader of the team! Leading the team all across the Galaxy! It's Brandon Falcon…"

"Catchy, huh?" Brandon said as he began to stun Virus right and left with the Stunderbuss. Ceres sighed as loud as she could as she ducked and rolled away from attacks.

"Helping the princess in saving her home!" the 'song' continued.

"Ooh, this is your part!" Brandon said as he swung the Stunderbuss into the face of a flanking Virus.

"From the evil Dr Quentin and…"

"He's not a doctor!" Ceres called as she waved her hand and deactivated a gun pointed right between her eyes.

"It's better for the song if he's a doctor!" Brandon said as he kicked back a grenade thrown in their direction. Three Virus troops scattered into various walls.

"Then there's Lenny, a robot with a gun! And there's Tia, who tags along for fun! And Ko'Tex, who doesn't have a gun!"

"You really can't write music, can you?" Ceres noticed as she wrenched the deactivated gun away and reactivated it in time to shoot the Virus in front of her in the leg.

"All the good themes were taken!" Brandon said as the sound of a pre-recorded Brandon making the sound of a guitar solo bellowed from his device. Moments later, the theme for *Teenage Mutant Ninja Turtles* began to play.

"Can we just get a move on?" Ceres called, opening the only closed door near them: one slightly out of the way on the other side of a group of Virus facing down the princess.

Brandon holstered his Stunderbuss and pulled out the Electro-Whip. He swung it and flourished it, making the Virus keep their distance lest they feel the full force of the whip's voltage.

"Our opening theme is over, I can be up for getting a move on," Brandon nodded.

Ceres groaned loud enough for Brandon to hear just how much of an inconvenience things were being. The bounty hunter spun all of his attention in her direction and began to flail the whip in the direction of the door.

"Is this the way we need to go?"

"I think I would know!" Ceres said, taking cover behind Brandon.

"Am I going to have to be the big strong bounty hunter who saves you from the scary people?" Brandon noticed.

If it were possible for Ceres' face to drop any further it would have. Instead she chose to just clap her hands together and let the bounty hunter watch two of the nearby walls come together and crush the Virus troops in front of them.

Brandon focused. "And why didn't you just open with that?"

Ceres rolled her eyes and tapped the bounty hunter's shoulder as she ran ahead.

"What about the rest of these guys?" Brandon said as he ran to catch up.

The music-playing device Brandon threw up to the ceiling fell back to the ground and exploded with a force that surprised even the bounty hunter. Ceres didn't bat an eyelash or even turn around. She just said "What guys?" as Brandon looked at the remaining Virus lying incapacitated on the ground.

"Whoa," Brandon said as he spun around before running after Ceres. "Hold up!"

After following Ceres deeper into Binary Castle, things began to look familiar. He knew what part of the building they were going to. The throne room.

Sure enough, the bounty hunter and the princess walked carefully towards the massive doors that led the very place Brandon was tasked to hunt down Ceres in the first place.

The princess looked up at the sheer height of the imposing doors and gulped.

"What's up?" Brandon said, on the lookout for any more Virus presence.

"This is it. This is where it could all go wrong."

"I see your faith in us getting this far hasn't disappeared."

Ceres turned and looked to the bounty hunter without a single extra word said, and with a gradual opening of her closed hand the throne room doors granted them entry.

It was not how Brandon remembered it to be. The gilded path towards the throne sat dull and flawed. The tapestries adorned across the walls hung tattered. All the precious stones that shone like stars in the ceiling had lost their lustre and their shimmer.

The throne room of the kingdom of Binary had become the origin of the planet's corruption. While the darkness and the exploitative consumption of what once was a perfectly untainted world spread its reaches little by little, the throne room appeared to be a catalyst. And sat at that throne the Virus stole from Binary through the massacre of the royal family and seizure of the crown was Quentin. Introduced to Brandon as the Steward to the throne, in reality he was the true usurper of the kingdom.

"Well, well," Quentin said, tapping on the once majestic seat that stood pride of place in the room. "It appears you have brought the princess back to us, *Falcon*."

Brandon took a step ahead of Ceres, obscuring her slightly from the Virus' gaze.

"You're a liar," Brandon said. "And a murderer, and you betrayed my honour."

Quentin laughed slowly and deeply. It sounded uncharacteristic for his slender form, but the captain knew he wasn't what he appeared to be.

"Brandon Falcon, I don't think you're in any position to take the high road."

The bounty hunter's hand rested on his Stunderbuss. He was ready for a fight.

"You weren't who you said you were. You wanted to kill a princess. And you wanted Binary all to yourself."

Quentin leant forward. His voice was definitely not the one Brandon first listened to. "And you think I don't already have this planet wrapped around my finger? This is just phase one. You just wait until our influence spreads. Where we'll go. Memtoria. Voxpo. Aurora. All the while, spreading…spreading our influence across the kingdoms and the governments and the barren lands and you won't even be able to touch us."

Brandon shook his head. "Well, I don't think you'll have the chance, Quentin. If that even is your name," he said as he held up his Stunderbuss. "The rightful Queen of Binary is back where she belongs and we brought friends to help stop you."

The princess cast a look around the throne room.

"Why is it just you? Surely you have guards," Ceres questioned.

Quentin laughed even more, shaking his head as he pulled himself out of the platinum throne. Step by step he descended to the level of the bounty hunter and the princess.

"Surely you've seen how well we Virus are at deception, *princess*?" Quentin said, cracking his fingers as he approached the duo, causing them to back away. "How we can easily change forms…"

The Virus' Binarian form shifted into the form of an Alliance officer before shifting into that of the Virus form Brandon saw Virgil take then back to Quentin's original appearance.

"We are not Binarians, this is true," Quentin bowed his head to Ceres. "You know who we are, but you are unaware of that we can do."

"I know how to stop you," Ceres said.

"Oh?" Quentin smiled the smile that made skin crawl and hairs rise.

"We took down Virgil. We've made nice work of your drones in the skies far above the planet. We've cut through your expendables to make it all the way here," Falcon smirked, triumphant.

"Funny," Quentin raised a finger and wagged it as he paced. "You say this 'we' a lot, and yet, I only see the two of you here before me. I thought you had a team?"

The Virus turned his back on the bounty hunter and the princess as he paced. Ceres put a hand on Brandon's to stop him striking immediately from behind. Quentin rounded back towards them, his head tilted down towards them, eyes glowing.

"As for Virgil, well…" Quentin began, before he began to split in half with each footstep. To his right, the slowly developing form of Virgil approached Brandon face-to-face. "He's easily replaceable."

"Ah," Brandon noted, staring down an exact replica of the Virus last seen rapidly leaving the Second Chance.

"So," Quentin bowed to the princess. "Shall we get this over with?"

Ceres withdrew a little from Quentin and Virgil. Even more so when Quentin's smile began to grow fangs as the Virus revealed his true form – similar to the form Virgil truly took but much, much bigger.

"Okay, next time I should be told exactly what I'm signing up for," Brandon said, cocking his Stunderbuss. "Because this is definitely not at all what I was expecting."

"And you think I was?!" Ceres said, opening her arms to try and find something to manipulate from the environment. She did not, however, get the chance, for a simple flick from Quentin sent the princess flying across the room, against the throne room's door.

"Screw it!" Brandon said, engaging Virgil in a fight by shooting at him several times with the Stunderbuss. Once again, things seemed to be ineffective. The bounty hunter still continued to persevere, strafing around the target, taking shot after shot after shot.

The much larger Quentin stalked his way over to the stunned princess. Everything practically shook with each time the Virus' foot slammed into the ground. Brandon even lost his balance from time to time as he tried to keep distance from Virgil's sharp claws.

Ceres, groggy, tried her best to get back up onto her feet. Her efforts were not helped by the constant shudder created by Quentin's approach. She didn't have the offensive capacity to deal with such a huge threat. Her eyes darted around to try and find something she could use to defend herself.

But she couldn't find anything.

That moment, a yellow blur flew over the grounded princess. Ceres managed to roll onto her back and see Ko'Tex travelling through the air above her; arms stretched ahead, claws drawn.

Quentin let out a pained roar as the Selenian's claws found their way home inside his chest. The Virus shook and attempted to shake the Selenian off, but Ko'Tex just kept pulling out his claws and stabbing them back inside the Virus, climbing up the giant antagonist.

Brandon's Stunderbuss continued to fire shot after ineffective shot against the defensive Virgil. He called out to Ko'Tex, "Oh now you want to arrive! You should have used a hoverboard!"

The Selenian didn't say a word back to Brandon in response, instead opting to headbutt Quentin. It did nothing, but it was worth a try. Ko'Tex's claws at least did a little damage to the lead Virus.

Quentin finally managed to get a grip of the dangling fugitive. Squeezing the Selenian with his claws, the Virus wrenched Ko'Tex away with a pained yell before tossing the Selenian against the wall. But he wasn't done yet. Quentin stumbled over to Ko'Tex and picked him up again, before tossing him upwards against the ceiling. The stones cut and ripped the Selenian's skin, a warm-up for the claws Quentin aimed underneath Ko'Tex, ready to slice and impale.

Ko'Tex fell downwards, straight towards the open claws of Quentin's hand, but before contact was made the Selenian was knocked off course. By Brandon's quick Stunderbuss shot. Ko'Tex tumbled along the ground away from Quentin once again while Virgil took the seconds of opportunity from Brandon's state of distraction to swing his own claws.

The Virus drew blood across Brandon's chest. His suit ripped open and the bounty hunter screamed in pain, instinctively clutching at the fresh wounds. Scarlet dripped over his golden gauntlets and onto his ineffective Stunderbuss as Virgil got closer and closer to make an even more effective strike.

Mere inches from doing so, Virgil was thrown to his right as if yanked strong and sudden in that direction. The loud sound of a sniper rifle immediately revealed the true cause. Tia looked around the scope of her gun as she made her way into the throne room. She fired again to keep the then retreating Virus at bay before noticing the even grander-looking Quentin hunched over Ceres and Ko'Tex.

"Brandon!" Tia yelled, her hands quickly dismantling part of her sniper rifle to create a less unwieldy version for close combat. "Use something that'll work against that guy!"

The alien tossed the gun over to Brandon, who holstered his Stunderbuss moments before snatching Tia's weapon from the air. The bounty hunter checked the ammo and took shot after shot against and around Virgil to keep him at bat.

Tia turned her attention to Quentin, who hadn't yet turned to face her. Reaching behind her with all four hands, the alien drew four different blades. With a nod, an exhale, and a cocky smirk, Tia nodded.

"I missed this."

She charged the Virus and began to spin like a top, her blades cutting and slicing around Quentin's legs. The Virus fell onto his knees as black ooze escaped his wounds, the alien continuing her aggression, striking at any free limb with her four armed limbs.

Ko'Tex and Ceres managed to stand up and centre themselves in the opportunities allowed to them due to Tia and Brandon's actions. Ceres ran around Quentin lest he attack her again while Ko'Tex checked the sharpness of his claws. He was ready to leap right back into the fray.

But leap he couldn't for something held him down to the ground.

The Selenian looked down at his feet, and noticed the spreading black ooze that had drained from Quentin's battle scars. It didn't take much intellect to know what something bad was afoot. To pardon a pun.

As if on cue, the ooze began to manifest into something else. More Virus. One for each of the crew of the Second Chance gathered in the throne room of Binary Castle.

Brandon turned his aim away from Virgil once again to take on the newly formed opponents, which is exactly when his opponent smacked the gun from out of his hands. Unarmed, Brandon raised his gauntlets and blocked another swipe from the Virus.

"Looks like you guys could use some help!"

L3-NY jumped into the throne room, throwing down a repulsor orb. The resultant effect of the gadget threw the smaller Virus in the room away from the group and left an opening between them and Virgil and Quentin just enough for Brandon and the others to scramble into a better position.

Lined up one against the other, the crew of the Second Chance held firm against the Virus. Quentin growled, his voice animalistic in his form.

"At least you get to die together."

"Nope," Brandon shook his head. "Not this time."

Brandon led the charge. Unarmed unlike the rest of his allies, Brandon swung towards the taunting Quentin. Meanwhile, Tia and L3-NY – with blades and dual-wielded guns respectively – engaged the smaller Virus forms while Ko'Tex full on attacked Virgil.

The Selenian embraced the advantage he soon gathered for himself, opting to ignore whatever restrictions of context and location he may have had beforehand. It was no longer a ship he was on, it was a planet. And a planet with a fair fight. No longer did the Selenian have to build on a reputation much lower than he fought for, the Binary Bounty gave him the challenge and the fight her felt he deserved.

The droid smelt money if he could actually smell as he took on a couple of the residual Virus. With the Binary Bounty so near to completion, the droid began to daydream of the ship he would buy with his riches. One that was asteroid proof. One that was like the Second Chance but more sleek and cool. Though it wouldn't have his old leg implemented as one of the ship's parts, L3-NY realised. A thought that then inspired a plan to try and buy the Second Chance from Brandon after their task was done that day.

The alien did what she felt she had to do. Having helped shape the person Brandon had become in the aftermath for the Battle for Aurora, the Binary Bounty seemed like a fitting 'one last job'. Despite training and working with the captain in the past towards a path of scum and villainy, the sheer fact that Brandon kept to a non-lethal code and stressed the need for help on a job involving helping a princess and eradicating those who were evil and without honour, well, Tia just had to tag along.

The bounty hunter had waited for a day like that day. Granted, he did not bet on the revelation of a corrupt life form in the System that could shapeshift and multiply at will, but the goal and the motivation was what he yearned for. The Binary Bounty did offer the promise of riches beyond anything he had seen or amassed before, but deep down he knew that wasn't what he was doing it for. And in the end, it wasn't for revenge against being betrayed by Quentin and the Virus. He knew exactly why the System brought together the crew of the Second Chance. And the answers were reflected in the ever-present golden gauntlets he had.

The left one of which Quentin's claws gripped around and squeezed. Tighter, tighter, tighter, before eventually, it shattered in a shower of microchips and servos.

"Oops," Quentin hissed. "I underestimate my own strength."

Brandon didn't feel a thing, of course, but his drive spurred him on to fight regardless of that setback.

"Still think you're the best bounty hunter in the System, don't you?" Quentin teased, his eyes flickering. "You bring three other bounty hunters along with you and still you aren't good enough."

The Virus grabbed Brandon by the neck and lifted him up. The others didn't have a chance to rush to his aid, their respective fights being the toughest they've faced so far. Quentin tutted and peered around.

"And it looks like the princess has run away," the Virus said, baring his fangs. "I guess you really have failed on your bounty, *Falcon*."

Brandon let out the best attempt of a laugh that he could before a loud bang filled the throne room.

Quentin relinquished his grip on Brandon's neck and stumbled back a second. In Brandon's right hand pointed a revolver gripped towards Quentin's chest. The barrel smoked.

The Virus stumbled backwards and touched his chest. "You…shot me."

Quentin began to shrink as he transformed back into his Binarian body. A look of shock kept on his face. He touched the point of entry and looked at the black blood staining his clothes and his fingers.

"You…you…" Quentin said, before breaking back into a smile. "You really thought that was going to hurt me?"

"Well, I…" Brandon scratched the back of his head.

"What, did you think that was going to *kill* me?" Quentin held open his arms. "Oh, Falcon, face it, you lost."

"My job was to get the princess here, so for that, I think I actually won," Brandon said, holstering his weapon. The bounty hunter raised his hand to show it was empty. "And I was never going to kill you."

The captain held his silence for a second before pointing behind Quentin. "But I have no say on what she does."

Quentin spun around to see the platinum throne Brandon pointed to. In it sat Ceres, who lit up the throne on her touch. With a smile and a wave, she lowered a crown object onto her head. The bounty hunter stepped away from Quentin and ushered back his friends.

"I have no idea what she's actually going to do," Brandon said to the others. "I still don't know what a technopath is."

Ceres did not leave them waiting long to see what she was actually capable of. At her touch with her rightful seat at the throne of Binary, the entire throne room began to glow. The lustre of the ground beneath their feet began to improve. Above them the star-like gems sparkled and reflected. Everything began to rebuild around them. The tapestries reformed. The light returned through the darkness. It was winning.

"Quentin. Or whoever you really are," Ceres said, her eyes glowing a bright blue. Her tone was more impactful than usual. Authoritative. Royal. "You committed heinous crimes against the crown of the kingdom of Binary."

Quentin drew his claws and grew into an even larger and formidable form than ever seen before. He continued to grow closer and closer towards the bejewelled ceiling. Stomp after stomp he ignored everything but the princess.

"You corrupted these lands. You planned to spread your evil deeper into the System. You eradicated the entire company of the Knights of Binary," Ceres listed, "And you killed my parents."

Quentin roared and flicked his claws. They seemed sharper. And deadlier. And all poised to strike Ceres at her throne.

"Your punishment…" Ceres said. "Is me."

Quentin ran towards Ceres as she slid her hands forwards and then flung them up into the air. Clenching her fists and drawing them back towards her, the princess released streams of white and blue energy. The beams cut through the room like fresh sunlight through the dying night. One by one they grew in number, and then overlapped, and then spread.

The Virus stopped its progression as the energy struck Quentin head-on. He raised his claws defensively, guarding his face as the power emanating from the throne continued. The lesser Virus forms didn't last so long. One after another, they exploded in a rain of black dust and smoke. Virgil inflated before he too was eradicated.

Brandon turned and looked out of the throne room from where they came from and noticed the corruption snaking its way from the throne room began to recede. The bounty hunter looked back towards Ceres, impressed, but also fearful of her true ability.

Quentin stayed exactly where he was, however. Ceres stood up and pointed. The floor began to roll and flip tile by tile towards the Virus before manipulating its way around Quentin's legs, trapping him in one place. Quentin swung his claws and gnashed his jaw as Ceres' continued onslaught increased. More and more light filled the room. Increasing numbers of energy beams shot from the throne and into Quentin.

Bit by bit, the Virus began to shrink in size. From the exaggerated form back into the form that just crushed Brandon's gauntlet. Then even smaller still, Quentin being forced to retake his form as a Binarian.

"You are not a Binarian," Ceres uttered. Even more energy shot from the throne, whipping up a storm.

Brandon shielded his eyes for a moment with his arm, his hand clutching at his open chest would. Ko'Tex and Tia hunkered down as L3-NY slid back against the wall.

Quentin yelled, helpless. "You can't do this to me!"

Ceres smirked. "I am the Queen."

Quentin shrunk smaller, and smaller still. No longer humanoid. No longer imposing. He shrunk as the brightness devoured the dark. Ceres walked over to where the Virus remained as almost everything as far as they could see shone brightly.

With a peek past his outstretched arm, Brandon saw the holo-dome redeploy in the distance. Buildings rebuilt. The black stretches of the Virus' grasp let go. Piece by piece, it disappeared.

Leaving the only trace of Virus in the room with the crew of the Second Chance and the Lost Queen of Binary Fields.

Ceres stood over the smallest spider. Black as the furthest, darkest reaches of space. Ceres looked down on it.

"I see we're both in our rightful place."

And she squashed the arachnid beneath her foot.

Stardate 2279.359

Binary had never looked better when Ceres reclaimed the throne. With the Virus presence on the planet eradicated, the newly appointed Queen made swift work of rebuilding.

It turned out that the throne and the crown catalysed Ceres' technopathic abilities. By infecting those artefacts Quentin – the anthropomorphic avatar of the Virus – allowed himself to rapidly cultivate and spread evil in the first place.

In Ceres' hands, however, she could manipulate and shape the landscape of the kingdom, returning equilibrium and utopia to her world.

"She really cleaned this place up well," Brandon said as he stood next to L3-NY.

"But at what cost?" L3-NY said, flicking a speck off his shoulder.

"Oh, I don't know, about a few million credits in care of some bounty hunters?"

"And a fugitive," Tia said, looking over to Ko'Tex.

"You fought well, Falcon," Ko'Tex said. "But do not forget our rematch."

"Yeah, love you too, Ko'Tex," Brandon said.

The four of them stood in the Hall of Ceremonies, a part of the Binary Castle scarcely used of late.

Across from them, as far as their eyes could see, Binarians stood. Genuine, appreciative Binarians. Under the Virus' rule, many went into hiding. Out of sight, out of mind. Fighting to survive as the corruption plagued their homeland.

"Nice turnout," L3-NY nodded.

Brandon smile beamed. "It's cos we're heroes."

"Pfft," Tia laughed. "Anti-heroes."

"Hey, we saved the day!" Brandon said as music played throughout the Hall.

"And got into a fight with the Alliance."

"*Multiple* fights with the Alliance," L3-NY corrected. "We even got into one on a prison convoy."

"You had a fight on a prison convoy?" Tia asked Brandon.

"Where they liberated me!" Ko'Tex added.

"Whoa, no," Brandon was quick to say. "You liberated yourself in that prison riot."

"Wait," L3-NY said. "What about all that Alliance above Binary?"
"Eh, they probably went home," Brandon shrugged it off.
"You sound so sure," Tia said.
"Do I? Wow, maybe I should have become an actor."
The Hall hushed as the doors opened with a loud creak. All the Binarians stood to attention as the crew of the Second Chance slowly stopped slouching when faced with the sight of the approaching Queen.
She held a small wooden box in her hands and beamed proudly at her friends. L3-NY waved, to which Tia pulled his hand down. Brandon waved too, which made Tia groan and eye-roll.
The procession music continued until Ceres made it up the steps towards the others.
She stood and turned back to her subjects.
"We are gathered here to honour the bravest people in the System."
"I feel like I'm getting married," L3-NY joked. Brandon chuckled. Tia forced an elbow into the droid to keep him quiet. "Whoa, Tia, not so rough…How about later?"
If the droid could have winked, he would have. Instead, one of his eyes switched off and back on again.
Ko'Tex shuffled on his feet. "Urgh, do I have to keep in one spot?" he noted the restrictive clothing he had on. "And did I have to wear this?"
"It's because you never wear appropriate clothes!" Brandon whispered.
Ceres raised her voice to combat the distracting whispering going on behind her.
"And now!" she said. "The medals!"
L3-NY spun his head. "Oooh!…I wonder how much I could sell mind for…"
"Brandon'll probably buy it," Tia offered.
"Hey!" the bounty hunter defended. "…But yeah, how much do you want?"
Ceres sighed and opened the wooden box. It glowed with the light of four holographic medals.
"For your courage, your bravery, your honour, your friendship, and the loyalty to your fellow crew, I award you all these medals for being heroes for our planet," Ceres decreed, going over to each of them and putting a medal around their necks.
Brandon held his medal in his recently reconstructed gantlet.

"Wow," the captain said. "I'm a hero."

"And you're really loud when I'm trying to be Queen," Ceres winked.

After the four heroes received their medals they stood to the applause of the Binarians. It felt good to each of them to be so appreciated.

"When…when do we leave?" L3-NY said. "This is getting pretty awkward just standing here."

"Yes, I need to get out of these clothes," Ko'Tex said.

"No!" the others all said.

Later, the group found themselves in the fully rebuilt Throne Room sharing a private audience with Queen Ceres.

"So, I guess you fulfilled your mission," Ceres said. "I thank you all so much."

"You were the one who saved the planet, princess," Brandon said.

"*Queen*."

Ceres smiled her crown shining atop her head.

"I rebuilt my home and my life has taken its next move. Yet I wouldn't even have that chance without all of your help," Ceres said. She walked over to the throne and raised her right arm. A sword formed from the floor and rose into her ready hand.

"Gah! She's going to kill us!" L3-NY said, patting for a weapon he relinquished to the royal guard. "With a sword! That would be so cool if she wasn't about to kill us!"

Ceres raised a hand to try and pacify him.

"Whoa, whoa, no, I wasn't going to kill you!" the Queen said. She held the sword in front of him. "Do you want to see it?"

L3-NY didn't need long to turn. "Yeah, sure. Sweet."

The droid walked closer to Ceres and took the sword. L3-NY did all manner of tricks with it before raising it back.

"Awesome."

"Lenny, come on, be professional," Brandon said. "…Can I have a go?"

Ceres sighed. "Of course."

After everyone had a chance with the sword – Ceres included – the Queen explained why she had the sword.

"I guess now that the bounty has been completed and paid in full you're all going to go on your separate ways."

"Well, Lenny wanted to get a new ship," Brandon noted.

"And Ko'Tex is still a fugitive on the run from the Alliance," Tia said.

"And they'll also be looking for Falcon," L3-NY said.

"And Tia and I shall have adventures together," Ko'Tex said.

"Will we?" Tia said, surprised as everyone else.

"You are a great warrior, and you are pleasing to my eyes," Ko'Tex nodded.

Surprised, Tia turned to Ceres to share a look. "Get in line," she said with a wink to the Queen.

Ceres smiled then looked across the assembled allies of her adventure around the system.

"Well, seeing as we are all here together for maybe the last time, I wanted to unite you all…" she said, raising the sword. "And Knight you…"

Brandon leant forward at those words. "Oh my god, I am going to become a Master of the Universe."

One by one, they kneeled as Ceres tapped their shoulders with the sword.

"I have the power," Brandon whispered on his turn.

"Arise," Ceres instructed the others. "Knights of Binary."

While almost purely ceremonial, the new title brought an air of feeling special and important.

"Sweet," L3-NY said, looking at his hands. "What does it pay?"

Ceres followed them out of Binary Castle and towards the newly built hangar where Brandon's ship was docked.

The captain grinned at the sight of the refurbished Second Chance. With his bounty, Brandon invested in improvements such as a lick of paint, completely new parts, and a finished interior all the way through the ship. No more exposed pipes and grated floors. The ship was more beautiful than it ever was before.

Brandon turned to the allies he had amassed on their quest as he stood in the shadow of his prized ship.

"Seeing as we have become these Knights of Binary…Which sounds like some *Voltron*, *G.I.-Joe*, *He-Man* sort of…" he said before noticing the blank expressions. "They're all cartoons. Come on, catch up. Anyway, since we've become this super team rag-tag gang of misfits – "

"Who are you calling misfits?" L3-NY said.

"What I'm saying is…" Brandon continued. "Why split up? We're the Knights of the Second Chance!"

"*Binary*," Ceres said.

"The Second Chance sounds so much better."

Tia shook her head. "You really are bad with your calls to action."

"Well we do need our rematch," Ko'Tex conceded.

"There we go! One!"

"I kinda have a kingdom to run," Ceres said. "But if you need a place to stay or you're just travelling through this part of the System, Binary shall be here for you."

"Do we get an allowance?" L3-NY asked.

Ceres just shook her head.

"Ah, well," the droid said. "I'll ride with you, Falcon. Until I can buy my new ride, at least. Unless you want to sell me yours?"

"Not a chance," Brandon said.

"How about giving me back my leg?"

Brandon refused to comment.

Tia patted everyone on the back at once. "Well I guess I'll join you too, Brandon. It'll be just like old times."

"That's the spirit!" Brandon clapped, and the ramp leading to the Second Chance lowered. "Cherry, prepare the ship. We're going on another adventure!"

"Where shall I plot a course to?" Cherry, the ship's A.I. asked.

"No idea, but I know the Alliance shall be after us every step of the way."

"Affirmative, captain."

"Oh Cherry, come on, you know that's not my name."

"You're right…*Fartbag*."

The bounty hunter grinned, surrounded by the gathered crew of the Second Chance. The Queen and her Knights of Binary.

"Cherry, start the playlist," Brandon instructed as they all walked up the ramp onto the Second Chance as Ceres waved them off.

"BRANDON FALCON!!!" yelled from the speakers as the ship's music began playing.

"That is not our theme song!" L3-NY shouted.

"Fine," Brandon accepted. "Cherry, play the next song."

And so began the *Darkwing Duck* theme.

Acknowledgements

The author would like to acknowledge:

Firstly, that even in a world 250+ years in the future and in a completely different System I still manage to reference Saturday Morning Cartoons from the 80s and 90s.

Secondly, that that and a whole bunch more of this book is a lot less scientifically sound than my previous book, *Cause and Effect*[1], and that dealt with superheroes and time-travel[2].

Thirdly, my parents. Who have been bumped up one place in the acknowledgements this time around. A writer needs someone to keep them on track yet shall at some point be annoyed with those people. But really, you got a book out of my head and onto the page. Again. Keep it up.

Fourthly, to my friends and colleagues, who have taken my parents place. Not as the people who raised me, but as those who have taken the fourth spot my parents had in the last book's thanks. Also, for you are rad, help reinforce my delusion of being a "writer", and are the first to buy my books. Sometimes.

Fifthly, to the once Edge of my Universe. I could write constellations about Us, but instead this is my final tribute to You. An entire galaxy. Without you the Lost Queen of Binary Fields would not exist, so for that, I thank you.

Sixthly, to the always-talented artist Jade Sarson, who once again has generated a fantastic and amazing book cover I could have only dreamt of until she drew it to life. (Find her stuff at http://www.teahermit.co.uk) Check out her stuff, she's going to be huge! She even has a graphic novel coming in 2016!

---

[1] Available now on Amazon!

[2] Seriously, it's worth checking out. It's on Amazon.

And finally, to You. The Reader. Again. Whether you've read my other stories or this is your first time, you're exactly who I'm writing for. Someone who wants to explore a whole new world. A new fantastic point of view. You are so special I made up those words on my own. Don't look it up.

But seriously, keep reading, and I'll keep writing. I'll still be writing if you stop, but you're going to be missing out on all the fun. Like more stuff like *Cause and Effect*!

About The Author

Christopher Francis was born in Ipswich, England and has never really left. Having graduated from the University of Lincoln and winning their 'Best Script Production Student' award in 2012, Christopher spends most of his current time writing, watching movies, and writing about watching movies.

The Binary Bounty is his third book. His prior novels Backwards From Infinity – a self-aware and thoroughly British take on the Young Adult genre – and Cause and Effect – a time-bending superhero adventure – are also available in paperback.

The author is currently working on other projects including his ninth feature screenplay and a couple new novels.

You can find some of his other work at http://www.awriterforhire.wordpress.com

You can also find him on Twitter @awriterforhire or on Tumblr at http://www.christopherfrancis.tumblr.com

He also has a Facebook, but he'd rather keep that for people he never interacts with.

Exclusive Preview of "The Keymaster" (Working Title), yet another work-in-progress by Christopher Francis

In a world both completely different from our one and almost exactly the same, in a time relative to ours yet simultaneously in the past and future, there lived a select few with the gifts of The Keymaster.

A Keymaster is one who can float between space and time through unassuming doorways that link the universes together, and they do this by using Keys.

Keys look no different than the ones in your pocket, on tables, in drawers, yet when they are used in certain locks…A whole new world is opened. Whether that world be in the past or future, Keymasters can drift between realities and parallel states, to explore, to live, to learn.

It wasn't long until Keymasters came under threat. Despite being a rather peaceful lifestyle, the essence of Keymasters' abilities led to the rather mischievous craving their abilities. To scour, to stalk, to steal.

Of a group in the hundreds soon cut down to a baker's dozen, Keymasters were essentially becoming extinct. Some had their Keychains stolen; some locked Doors and threw away their Keys; some purely died without revealing their secrets.

By the time the Lockpicks narrowed their search to Tariq Stan, they had managed to crudely replicate the effect of the Keymasters' Keys, but it was not a perfect art.

But they were capable enough to chase Tariq through time and space, desperate to steal his Keychain.

Tariq threw open his fifth door, a couple of Lockpicks almost immediately on his tail. He found himself in what was to him a futuristic land, where vehicles floated in the air and food was advertised to be in a new cubic form.

He sprinted through a building parallel to the city's 5 lane-high streets, whipping around desks and chairs, knocking over anything and everything he could to try and slow his aggressors down.

As he dived out of the room and rounded a corner to continue running through the hall, he glanced back at the people chasing him.

Lockpicks were physically no different to Tariq, but they dressed in garments of black and gold, shielding their identities behind masks. Lockpicks did not possess the rattling Keychain full of Keys like Tariq had, but instead had all manner of implements forged to do similar things.

Tariq could make out the unmistakable outline of a Ram in one Lockpick's hands, while a glint in the sunlight revealed that the other had Picks on him.

Wherever Tariq was going to go, they could follow.

Despite this prospect of eternal chasing across the universes, Tariq reached for his hip. There, he found his Keychain. With the many Keys jangling around the silver halo of metal, Tariq activated the Burn function that was built as a countermeasure for his Keys.

For every Key he used, they would now melt in the lock. One use only. One way. With this implemented, even if Tariq lost his Keys, the Lockpicks couldn't exploit them for their own personal gain. They'd be lost in an endless cycle until the Keychain ran out of usable Keys. From there, they'd be forever lost to time and space, never to return home.

Tariq kept an ace up his sleeve, however. One final key that he could use as a last resort. To take him home. Right back to where his journey started, but hopefully with no Lockpicks on his tail.

But it was a last resort.

He still had many cards to play.

"Give us the Keychain, and we'll let you go!" shouted one of the Lockpicks.

Tariq panted and breathed as he continued to run. Lockpicks don't just let Keymasters go after catching them. Once they get your Keys, you're expendable.

"There's no use!" Tariq yelled, sweat beading down his temple. "My Keys are useless to you!"

The other Lockpick yelled. "Then give us the Keychain and no-one will get hurt!"

There's something not quite right, Tariq thought. His eyes darting around, he realised that it was just himself and the Lockpicks in the general vicinity.

The world he had entered was empty.

Except for the Doors around him that began to open, revealing even more Lockpicks.

“Oh dear,” Tariq muttered. He came to a stop and spun in a circle.
Tariq was surrounded.
So he had to escape.
He dove to his left, towards a cleaning cupboard in the building he was in. Tariq rummaged through his Keychain for a Key that would fit the lock and use the portal that would be created going through the door.
From all directions, Lockpicks were coming. As the Keymasters’ numbers dwindled, Lockpicks were amassing. They were gaining a strong hold over most of the Doors.
They could never have them all, however. Tariq pondered this as he managed to unlock a Door and stepped through it. Keymasters once had infinite potential, but that potential was long squandered. Many secrets were lost as Keys and Keymasters were lost, and not even the most dangerous of Lockpicks could unlock that potential once more.
If anything, Lockpicks had the ability to travel between a limited range of locations – ones where stolen Keys could take them. Keys were simple and complex like that.
They could steal Tariq’s remaining Keys, but if they could not steal Tariq, the Keymasters would not entirely fail the universe.
It is with this knowledge that Tariq took as comfort. And as motivation, for as he found himself in a Renaissance-era cathedral, Tariq maintained an effort to break away from his pursuers.

There were fewer Doors in the cathedral. This meant that less Lockpicks had the potential to slip through the cracks. Tariq looked around and found himself in a strange land. Religions were not as conventionally practised from where he came from, not in the least the religion he practised.
Keymastery was not a religion, nor a cult. It exercised a freedom to religion, but once one travels through the universes in the way a Keymaster does, what one believes soon becomes something entirely different.
Due to the fact that religion has and always will be a touchy and most complicated subject to discuss and contemplate, Tariq didn’t reflect too much on that aspect on his surroundings.
Nor did he hold the actions going on around him against the religious institution he was in. For the hooded inhabitants who Tariq thought were in prayer soon turned on him.
Because he had found himself in a Lockpick stronghold.

It was not, as Tariq reflected, the most ideal location for him to be in at that moment in time. And considering that, he looked around for an exit.

"Give us the Keys!" Lockpicks continued to shout.
"Over my dead body!" Tariq rebuffed.
Lockpicks began drawing the tools of their trade – aggressive tools. Tariq stood strong. It was true; they would never get those Keys unless he was dead or otherwise gone.
And Tariq wanted to be gone.
The remaining Keys on his Keychain were already dwindling. He made calculations, and he made a break for the nearest Door.
Key after Key melted in the locks as Tariq tried to escape. But a couple of Lockpicks held their chase. One particularly hefty Lockpick used brute force to reopen the Doors Tariq used. With a Ram, Lockpicks could burst through Keymaster Doors, however irreparable damage caused by it meant it was still only one way.

Tariq dipped and dodged around Victorian London, where he used the overcrowded buildings to lose a few of his pursuers. Burning a Key in the Door of a factory, Tariq found himself in the Tokyo of 2055, where robotics had been perfected, but also rebelling against the locals.
It was here where Tariq lured a handful more of his aggressors into a trap, where Lockpicks where surrounded by aggressive robotic fast food servers.
A dozen Lockpicks remained by the time Tariq found himself in the Times Square of New Year's Eve 1999, and even as the ball dropped, the masked antagonists continued their chase.
All manner of kissing and hugging and marriage proposals that happened around Tariq meant that the whole world was oblivious in that moment of a Keymaster in mortal peril as evil Lockpicks continued their strife, and in a way, that was alright by Tariq. Why conjure worry and distraction at such a happy time of human history? And for Tariq, he was just annoyed he couldn't spend more time in that world, for he had never been to that time.
And probably never will.
Though it was the hope that he could return that spurred him on. While the Lockpicks were out for his blood, Tariq kept optimistic. He was not the first to be chased like this, and it wasn't the first time he himself was chased, so he picked up a few things.

Such as the melting keys.

But he didn't prepare for having next to no keys on his person.

Or more specifically…Just one.

Tariq saw the end in sight: An unassuming Door at the end of quite a foreboding alleyway. It was dark, it was shady, but it was the last path he could take.

As seconds continued to tick into the year 2000, Tariq was running out of time. Lockpicks were on his tail, and if he didn't take the Door that had presented itself to him, Tariq would be running out of life, too.

Therefore, Tariq dived into the alleyway.

And a Lockpick managed to dive on him.

Sliding across the concrete floor, Tariq was tackled by a burly Lockpick who got him around the ankles. More Lockpicks were approaching, but for those few moments, it was just Tariq and the one aggressor.

The Door laid mere steps out of reach.

Tariq kicked, and he wriggled, trying whatever he could to get free of the Lockpick. The Keymaster flailed his legs, his feet slowly slipping out of the grasp of his antagonist.

Others were closing in.

Tariq rolled a meter or two away from the one in the alley with him, but the Lockpick was already on his feet. Tariq pulled himself up, and braced, and in a snap the Lockpick collided with him once again, the force pushing him up against the door.

Tariq slammed his fists into the Lockpick's back while the enemy lifted him. He clapped the Lockpick's temples, dazing him for a second. And only for a second.

A hand gripped around Tariq's neck. It squeezed. Air gushed out of Tariq; air that wasn't soon replaced. Tariq whipped at the arm on him, but it wasn't enough.

The Lockpick raised a Ram. It wasn't about to be used on a Door, though.

But rather, Tariq's face.

The Keymaster rummaged quickly.

One final Key on the Keychain.

Tariq slammed it into the nearby Lock. Twisted it. As it began to melt in the Lock, the Door swung open, allowing Tariq through.

And the one Lockpick.

The Door slammed shut behind them as Tariq was thrust into a cart carrying food. Tariq grabbed a nearby tray of food and swung it at the sole Lockpick. It connected, stunning his aggressor, but soon both were thrown off balance.

It wasn't another building or a street they had found themselves in.

It was a plane.

A passenger jet, to be exact. Some decades after the turn of the century they had just come from. And it wasn't empty. If anything, it had sold more seats than it actually had.

The travellers had found themselves in a vessel full of innocent people, whom were quickly thrown into potential chaos with the conflict erupting around them.

In this entire endeavour to escape, Tariq pondered just how many guidelines he had broken to get to this point, and then he pondered just how many he was going to in the future.

It was a lot, but an exact number was impossible to fathom.

But it probably could be better answered with "Most of them".

People gasped, people screamed. Tariq threw curious gazes around his immediate surroundings, but that was only for a second.

For turbulence hit.

Both Tariq and the Lockpick were thrown around as the plane rattled, shook, leapt, and dropped. Punches were thrown, and some hit, but others missed.

The two continued to be locked in mortal combat – neither of them with any real way to get back or get anywhere that wasn't where they were – that was, until the fasten seatbelts sign switched off.

Then an air marshal was on them.

More accurately, an air marshal was on the Lockpick, nabbing the aggressor from behind. In a headlock, the Lockpick reached for a Ram that was no longer there, but instead sat in Tariq's hand.

The confusion was enough for Tariq to do some stealing of his own. Temporarily of course.

He gave it back. Directly to the Lockpick's face.

There was a horrible crunch, and a nose was probably broken, but nothing time and medical attention couldn't fix.

As the Lockpick crumpled to the floor, hopefully out for the count, the Air Marshal got Tariq in his sights.

His gun sights.

Tariq knew better than most of the general population of any time that had lived with air travel that shooting a gun on a plane wasn't *always* a recipe for explosive decompression, but he still didn't take his chances.

The only chance he took was that the Marshal wasn't going to shoot immediately on sight, and it was a chance well took. For yet another bout of turbulence hit.

Tariq stumbled and bashed against seats as he pulled his way through the cabin towards the front of the plane, the Air Marshal all the more ready to take him down one way or another. The Keymaster reached for whatever was near so he could throw it towards the law enforcer: hand luggage, in-flight magazines, tiny bottles of alcohol…And for the most part, it worked as a distraction.

But only a distraction. The Marshal continued his approach.

Tariq finally made it to as far front as he could on the plane. He was stopped only by the locked door to the cockpit, and hindered by the continued pursuit of the Air Marshal.

"That's quite far enough," the Air Marshal said to Tariq. He raised his badge and aimed his gun at The Keymaster. "US Air Marshal. You're under arr–"

Those were the only words Tariq said, because the Marshal in that instant was taken out. By the Lockpick.

A huge thud from the Lockpick's Ram knocked the Marshal out in such a way that Tariq assumed it was a little more than knocking someone out, and as the officer hit the floor, Tariq knew his time was up.

The Lockpick approached. Step by step. Ram in hand. No turbulence around to save Tariq any more.

Closer.

His antagonist was almost on him yet again. It was the end. Tariq had no more tricks up his sleeve.

But he did have one around his neck.

The Keymaster whipped his hand under the top of his shirt, reaching for the necklace he wore. He spun towards the door to the cockpit. There was no way the pilot, co-pilot, or any air hostess was going to open it for him to escape.

He would have to open it himself.

Even though it was the riskiest, most dangerous option he could have picked.

But with his life on the line and with both his and the Keymasters' interests at best, Tariq pulled his necklace off, revealing the oldest Key in his possession. The one Key all Keymasters possessed.

The Key to The Hub.

Both weighty and feather-light; between a real object and an impossible creation; colourless, dark, yet so distinctive, the Key Tariq held in his hand had the potential to be the most dangerous thing in the universe.

And the Keymaster put it inside the nearby Lock, twisted it around three times anti-clockwise, pressed against the Door, and entered.

Except what wasn't supposed to happen was what happened to the Keymaster immediately afterwards.

For one thing, a Pick went into Tariq's hand, thrown by the Lockpick as a last ditch attempt to stop him.

Another, the Key snapped in the Lock. Which didn't create the same effect as a Key that melted.

Because Keys that snap mid-transition mean something has malfunctioned.

And when that happens to the Key to The Hub, well.

The Universe has to compensate.

Printed in Great Britain
by Amazon.co.uk, Ltd.,
Marston Gate.